Yvonne

Hathaway House, Book 25

Dale Mayer

YVONNE: HATHAWAY HOUSE, BOOK 25
Beverly Dale Mayer
Valley Publishing Ltd.

ISBN-13: 978-1-778860-24-9
Print Edition

Books in This Series:

Aaron, Book 1

Brock, Book 2

Cole, Book 3

Denton, Book 4

Elliot, Book 5

Finn, Book 6

Gregory, Book 7

Heath, Book 8

Iain, Book 9

Jaden, Book 10

Keith, Book 11

Lance, Book 12

Melissa, Book 13

Nash, Book 14

Owen, Book 15

Percy, Book 16

Quinton, Book 17

Ryatt, Book 18

Spencer, Book 19

Timothy, Book 20

Urban, Book 21

Victor, Book 22

Wesley, Book 23

Xavier, Book 24

Yvonne, Book 25

Zander, Book 26

Boxed Sets and Bundles

https://geni.us/Bundlepage

About This Book

Welcome to Hathaway House. Rehab Center. Safe Haven. Second chance at life and love.

Yvonne made a mistake leaving Hathaway House and walking away from Dennis. Hugely comforting and caring man that he was, she had been so determined to move forward and to be someone independent that she couldn't see what he had to offer. Until it was too late.

Dennis could only love and let her go years ago. Now she's returned to Hathaway House—injured again, broken inside, emotionally devastated, and worn out from the hard fight she has endured over the last five years. And Dennis is forced to the sidelines, watching as the woman he loves once again struggles to work toward her new more-broken reality.

If only she could see this as a second chance for both of them …

Sign up to be notified of all Dale's releases here!
https://geni.us/DaleNews

YVONNE BRITMAN STOOD outside the front doors of Hathaway House. Lord, this was not how she wanted to return. When she'd left, she had been in tears, a broken woman in so many ways, and yet one put back together in so many other ways. She'd been so determined to be someone—someone new. Someone who could handle the changes in her life, prepped to be a success regardless of physical injuries. She'd been so sure she could rise to the top …

As she stood here for a long moment staring at the entrance, a woman opened up the door and asked, "Are you coming inside? Would you like some help?"

Yvonne smiled and nodded, and, using her arm crutches, made her way slowly up the ramp.

"Most of the time," the woman noted, "people come by ambulance."

"I was really hoping not to," Yvonne replied.

At the sound of her voice, the other woman gasped. "Oh my. Yvonne?"

Dani. Yvonne let Dani's arms wrap around her in the gentlest of hugs, bringing tears to her eyes. "As much as I love you guys to bits, I really, really, *really* didn't want to come back here."

"Not like this, I'm sure," Dani noted. "However, anytime we can help a former graduate of this place, we're here for them. When you called back about the IT interview, your request to return as a patient was not what I expected."

"Well, a car accident was not what I expected to happen either."

"Nor being on a crosswalk," Dani added. "You certainly didn't have to drive yourself here today."

"Yet it was hard for me *not* to," she replied. "I … I left this place. I left it in good conscience. I left it thinking that I was done with rehab forever. And yet here I am."

"I'm not sure if anybody's injuries are ever healed forever," Dani clarified. "So don't put that pressure on yourself," she whispered.

As Yvonne made her way into the front lobby, she collapsed onto the nearest chair, the shudders racking through her body.

"And, of course, you did too much already," Dani scolded her.

"No, just a show of pride. Stiff, ugly, cold-at-night pride."

Dani winced. "I haven't told him, you know?"

She nodded. "That's probably for the best. He'll see me when he sees me, and we'll deal with it then."

"Are you sure?" Dani asked. "If it were me, I would want a little bit of notice."

"Nope, maybe we'll hash it out this time around."

"I hope so," Dani said. "He's a good man."

"He's the best, but that didn't mean it was right to leave at the time."

"That's for you guys to figure out," Dani suggested. "In the meantime, I'm so sorry for what happened to bring you back to us, but you're here now, and we'll help. We will take care of you."

Yvonne looked up at her old friend and nodded slowly. "And you have no idea how grateful I am for the opportunity to come back."

"Even with Dennis here?" Dani teased.

"Maybe especially because Dennis is here," she admitted, with a nod. "It's time. Whether that guy knows it or not, it's time."

"Good luck with that. Dennis is many things, but I know he cares for everybody else first. His needs come dead last."

"Well, this time," Yvonne declared, "he just might have to deal with his own feelings because I'm not going away. Not again."

Chapter 1

YVONNE STOOD STILL and stared out the window of her private room. The sun was barely up, and the world was silent. She had survived her first crazy day back here, even if only part of a full day. She couldn't believe that she was once again at Hathaway House, after all the hard work she'd put in to get out of here last time. However, she was grateful to even be back again and to have these resources available to her, and yet how did that work now?

She swore when she left five years ago that she would never return, and yet, apparently, one should never make those kinds of promises. She had not seen Dennis, but she knew he was here. The grapevine had probably already filled him in. She didn't even know how to approach him. Her nerves kicked in at the thought. They hadn't left on good terms, and that was her fault. She had been so full of herself, and so full of the need to go on and to prove that she was fine and capable and able to be on her own, that she'd basically run from here to her future alone—certainly not considerate of anyone else's feelings, especially Dennis's. And now look.

It was only the beginning of her first full day back, and she already felt that same sense of helplessness that she'd felt before. And she hated it, absolutely hated it.

Nothing was worse than knowing that life was passing

you by and that she could do nothing about it. Of course nobody else had seen that life was passing her by. They all didn't understand that deep urge for her to prove that she was somebody. That drive to take control. She never even noticed the *life passing her by* part. She certainly never let go of the control part. And yet, now, she couldn't necessarily do anything about either.

Life sometimes just dealt you lemons, and, even though Dennis would say, *Make lemonade*, it didn't always work out that way. She'd been so sure that she could move on with life and could do great on her own. And honestly, she had. She didn't have any reason to feel as if she had failed in that, but, because she was back at Hathaway House again, it sure felt like a failure.

She could have moved faster and missed that vehicle, yet being on the crosswalk at that moment in time was almost a message saying, *Ha, you're not that good. See? We just proved it.*

Her prosthetic had slowed her down.

She'd also not been doing her exercises, hence slowing down her reaction times. *Ugh.* That was really hard to accept too. She was all about success, so why had she failed to do her follow-up exercises? Sure, she'd been crazy busy, but that was no excuse.

She didn't really want to deal with that whole sense of failure all over again, but what did one do except deal? This was the hand she had been dealt, so that's what she would do. When a man spoke from her doorway, she stilled. She didn't even know how to react. She slowly turned, using the windowsill for balance.

Dennis leaned against the doorjamb, his arms crossed over his massive chest.

She looked at him, nodded. "Hey, Dennis."

"Hey," he replied, but he didn't enter, and neither did she invite him in.

He nodded slowly, as if acknowledging the huge space between them. "How're you doing?" he asked, still from the doorway. "I heard the trip was pretty rough."

"All trips are pretty rough right now," she admitted.

"And a drunk driver hit you?"

"Apparently. I was on the crosswalk, but my reaction time wasn't there."

"You're still taking the blame for everything, *huh*?" He stepped forward.

Her eyes widened. "Is that what I'm doing?" she asked in a mocking tone.

He shrugged. "Sounds like it to me. Are you thinking that you could have avoided it?"

"I was thinking that, if my reaction time had been a bit better, I would have dodged getting hit."

"Not likely," he noted. "You seem to be having some rough days. Maybe several nights too."

"I can't say I've had much chance to catch my breath since I got here."

"At the change in circumstances, or at being back here again?"

He was always blunt, and you always knew exactly where you stood with him. "Both, I guess. I'm grateful to be back, grateful to be in the hands of the people who can help me again." She sighed, adding a small smile. "I'm also sad to be back and so very sorry to be in this situation again, where I thought I was done."

"I believe one of the things you said was, *Sayonara, this was it*, and how you were never coming back again."

"That's what happens when you're a fool," she stated, trying hard to mask her bitterness.

"You still drink coffee?"

"I do." She eyed him hopefully. "Any chance of a cup?"

"I can get one for you," he offered. "You didn't eat last night."

"No, traveling is pretty rough on me these days."

"Stomach issues?"

She shrugged. "It's a mix of missing body parts and the painkillers, which still knock me for a loop and nauseate me."

"Ah, so do you want any food to go with your coffee?"

She stared down at her cell phone. "It's too early yet. It's only 6:00 a.m." She frowned at him. "How come you're even here?"

"Why not?" he replied. "I tend to live here these days."

She stared at him. "And yet you're the one who tells me that I'm a workaholic."

"I *am* a workaholic," he confirmed cheerfully.

This was more like the old Dennis Yvonne knew, instead of that *first-awkward-meeting* Dennis.

He added, "It doesn't change the fact that I do what I do because I love it."

She nodded. "That's what I thought I was doing too," she noted, "until life, for a second time, wiped me right out."

"Let me get you that coffee." And he disappeared, his footsteps striding confidently down the corridor.

That was one of the things that she'd always had trouble with. His inner sense of knowing, understanding that what he was doing in his life was where he needed to be and what he needed to do. She hadn't had that same confidence in her life. She hadn't had anything like it.

She'd loved him to distraction but couldn't stay for him, so what did that say about her? Deep down she knew that he had loved someone else, his true love dying early. Yvonne knew better than to fight a losing battle with a dead lover turned into some perfect saint. Yvonne finally let go of that, realizing her own lack of self-confidence was the real culprit.

She'd spent a lot of time over the last few years on her solo journey thinking about the choices she'd made. It had only been five years, but, man, just catching sight of him this morning was enough to make her heart break. And more than that, it was enough to see the distance in his own gaze and to realize that so much had changed between them.

Maybe not enough and maybe too much. She had a lot of making up to do. And, even at that, she wasn't sure she could get anything out of this attempt except forgiveness. Yet she would take even that right now.

She still had to focus on her rehab journey now, the same as last time. Previously she'd been determined to make it on her own, positive that nobody else could help her, that nobody else was of the same mind-set, so they didn't know what she was going through and couldn't possibly understand. To say she had been a fool was so obvious today, but she had been oblivious to that fact before.

And now, here she was back again, and all she could think about was how she could not do it alone. This time she desperately wanted to have somebody by her side, for the days that went bad, for the nights that got terrible—even more so when she felt everything was wrong in the world and where someone would need to encourage her to keep trying, even when she would rather give up.

This time, in so many ways, was worse than last time. It shouldn't have been. It should have been a triumph for

Yvonne to successfully walk back into Hathaway House as a new employee, not a returning rehab patient. She'd retrained in the IT field, knowing in the future that her leg and prosthetic would give out on her, and she didn't want to retrain into yet another career down the road.

Now she was quite a programmer, which was great, but a lot of her life was empty. She'd spent so much time struggling to get back on her feet, to return to the world as a full-time wage earner, to get back to being independent—both financially as well as physically. However, all she'd found in her previous five years was how so much of her life was one thing and one thing only. *Empty.*

DENNIS HEADED TO the kitchen. He stared down at his trembling hands. He'd known that Yvonne had arrived last night and had checked with the nurse to ensure Yvonne was okay. But to see her today, to see that beaten look on her face, was heartbreaking. For the umpteenth time he cast his mind back to how they'd left it and how she needed to leave. Even though he wanted to say so many things to make her stay, he also knew that she wouldn't, that she couldn't, that she had to go.

Now she was back, and what did that mean for him? Possibly nothing.

With a loud sigh, he shook his head. He had only known romantic love two times in his life. His first love had died young, leaving Dennis thinking that was his one and only chance. He still loved her to this day. He easily acknowledged that to himself and others. Yet he was wise enough to not make her into a glorified saint, a perfect woman with no flaws, as too many people do when a loved one passes on. Truly that hadn't been a problem, once he met Yvonne. Both of his loves were true loves, but each woman was totally different and distinct.

Yvonne was his current love and probably would remain in his heart for the rest of his life. He couldn't and wouldn't force Yvonne to feel the same way about him. That was totally up to her. That was what made falling in love so heady, so awesome, and so terribly frightening as well. Talk about making oneself totally vulnerable. That's what love was about.

The only thing he could do was be himself and see how she felt about him this time around.

Dennis, in his innate wisdom, knew that changing himself to be better for another person didn't ever work out. You had to change for you. You had to be you, honest and authentic to yourself. If you were lucky, the people in your life returned the favor by being honest and authentic back. And Yvonne certainly had been that way back then.

However, what she'd wanted was so different than what Dennis saw them sharing together that he had been forced to walk away and to just let it be. Just let her be. It had been hard. Watching her leave broke his heart. Now here she was back again. Not to see him, not because she was a success and came back to be their full-time IT person, proving how well she'd done solo out in the big wide world. Nope, she was here because she was broken again. And that was even harder for Dennis to see.

At the kitchen he quickly poured her a cup of coffee and looked at the food currently available, wondering if she needed something until the full breakfast was served. It was early definitely, but not so early that he couldn't get her something if that's what she needed. Still, she hadn't exactly made her choices clear. And, for the first time, hesitant and doubting himself, he just snagged a muffin full of lots of seeds and nuts and put it on a plate for her and carried it back to her, along with her black coffee.

The whole time he stared down at his hands, wondering what he would do about his shaky reaction. Everybody would know, just as everybody had known last time. But now Hathaway House was so much bigger, so much crazier here, with more staff and more patients. Yet, for all Hathaway House's growth, all these people remained a tight-knit family. So everybody would keep watch over everybody else—something he hadn't personally had to experience, except for many years ago.

So now he would be in prime position for everybody else to watch him and to see how his renewed relationship with Yvonne unfolded. In a way, it was only fair. He'd watched so many relationships in these last several years, but they'd all worked out. Only Dennis's relationship with Yvonne had gone off the rails.

Giving himself a stern talking to, he continued to her room and knocked gently on the door. When he heard her voice, slow and heavy, he opened the door and stepped in, asking, "Are you all right? Do you need a nurse?"

She tried to shake herself awake. "I dunno. I might just need to sleep some more."

"In that case, I won't give you the coffee."

She stared at the cup, steam coming off the top. "Just leave it. If I can drink it, I will," she murmured. "Otherwise …"

"Otherwise," he interrupted, "you'll just fall back asleep, and that's what you need primarily." He carefully put both items on the bedside table. "I brought a muffin, just in case you get snacky."

"Ah, Dennis," she muttered. "Still looking after everybody."

"Sure," he replied in a casual tone. "I enjoy being of service, like the rest of the staff here."

"You were always too good to be true."

He wasn't sure if the drugs were talking or something else. "Did the nurse just bring you a painkiller?"

She shifted in bed, her eyelids falling closed. "Yes. I wasn't expecting it to knock me out quite so fast."

"Seems you need it," he murmured. "So just rest." And he backed up to the door.

"I'll do that," she muttered, but her words were slurred, as she turned her head to the side.

He saw her drop off again. He wasn't sure that this was even normal. As he looked up the hallway, one of the nurses exited a room close by, and he asked her, "Yvonne's out again. Is that okay?"

The nurse nodded. "She's pretty exhausted and in a lot of pain."

He frowned at that. "I was hoping her pain wasn't so off-the-wall."

"I'm hoping it'll get better too," the nurse shared. "I guess you two know each other, don't you?"

"Yeah." He gave a hard sigh. "She was a patient here a long time ago."

"Let's hope we can get her back on her feet and back out into the world again," she murmured. "It's got to be hard to return to rehab."

Funny how he'd never really thought about that angle, but maybe it was. Maybe that was part of the problem here.

Maybe it just felt like a failure to her, which was something she didn't handle very well.

"Hopefully she'll be much better after this," the nurse added, with a gentle smile. "Let her sleep."

And, with that, he returned to the kitchen and was greeted with a sudden silence, as if everybody had been talking about him. He turned around and addressed everybody, "Yes, I did have a previous relationship with her. Yes, I'm sad that she's back because I know it means she's hurt. No, I have no idea what it means for us, where any relationship with Yvonne will go. So a little respect and a little time to adjust would be helpful." And, with that, he left the kitchen.

Ilse followed him and explained, "We weren't talking about you." He frowned, as he studied her silently. "They just knew that somebody had come in who'd had a previous relationship with someone," she told Dennis. "After you walked out, I gave them a quick explanation."

He sighed. "And, of course, I've just made it so much worse, haven't I?"

She smiled. "No, not at all. You have to remember, not everybody has been here as long as you and I have. So, a lot of people don't have a clue how much we all went through when we first started here."

"No, you're right," he murmured. "It just seems so different right now. Yet seeing her again? It's as if we were never apart these last five years."

"Do you need to take off for a couple days?" she asked him, eyeing him carefully.

"No, I don't. And I'm sorry. I shouldn't have jumped the gun in there."

"It just shows me how rattled you are by all this."

"Sure," he conceded. "How would you feel if you found somebody again who you loved?"

"Terrified, scared, nervous, exuberantly euphoric."

"I feel all those things," he admitted, "but not the euphoric part because she left, because she didn't want anything to do with me."

At that, Ilse frowned. "I do remember her leaving. I'm not sure she was rejecting you as much as proving to herself that she could do this, could graduate from Hathaway House and could make it in real life. Her leaving was pretty tough back then. It was tough on all of us because we all hurt for you."

"And yet it was the right thing for Yvonne to walk away," he noted. "It was what she needed to do."

"And you let her go, thinking of her desires over your own," Ilse pointed out. "Whether that was smart or not, I don't know."

"Neither do I," he stated, a sadness in his soul. "I know she's back, but I also know it's not where she wants to be. She's not back here for me."

"And yet what you aren't privy to this time," Ilse stated, "is where she's at mentally right now. For all you know, everything has changed in her world. Maybe she's looking for something completely different."

"Maybe," Dennis muttered, "but, once again, she's traumatized and in a tough space, so what she really needs is support, but with no commitments."

"Don't decide what she needs before she has a chance to tell you what she needs," Ilse noted, with a gentle smile. "I think this is a very different woman here at present than who was here last time," she shared, "if for no other reason than she has learned and grown a lot from being out in the big bad world."

He frowned at her and then nodded. "You could be right there. … Still, I know she's not after anything from me. Otherwise she could have come to me at any point in time in the last five years."

"Remember though," Ilse added, "as a matter of pride, it's very hard to reopen a door you closed. Whether she wants to open it or not, it's a, … it's a hard thing to do. It's a hard thing to face. She may see it as admitting she's a failure. So she may let it slide day in and day out, until, all of a sudden, it's too hard to open that door because you have no reason, no explanation or excuse as to why … you didn't do it earlier," she explained calmly. "So maybe just relax and let things naturally happen between you two, without precon-ceived ideas or some timetable. If you are meant to be with Yvonne, it's meant to be. If it's *not* meant to be, well, I'll sit here and commiserate with you all over again."

He winced at that. "That's not a memory I want to re-visit."

She chuckled. "But we went on baking sprees that were a lot of fun."

He grinned at her affectionately. "Only you would think baking sprees were a lot of fun."

"Hey, we came up with some great recipes, and it was a good way to get your mind off everything else that was going on."

"It was at that." Dennis opened up his arms, and she stepped in, and they hugged gently for a moment.

"Remember," she whispered, "that Yvonne's hurt, she's injured, and what she needs right now is a friend."

He nodded. "Being a friend is something I'm good at. I just, one day, had thought maybe I would be more than a friend."

"And you don't know that it won't be. Give her space, give her time, and see what she wants for herself."

"Will do." He sighed. "And now is that food ready? 'Cause, boy, oh boy, I can hear the animals in the cage outside."

Ilse burst out laughing. "Breakfast is ready. Let's get it moving."

Chapter 2

YVONNE WOKE UP a short time later, feeling a little groggy but more refreshed. She shifted in the high-tech hospital bed and shuddered as the pain skittered up her spine.

Almost immediately she heard someone say, "I saw that."

She looked over to see Shane in her doorway. "Coming here, I wondered if your still being here was a good thing or a bad thing," she admitted, with half a smile. "You made my life better in so many ways, and yet the rehab process was not easy."

"Sorry," he replied, "none of this process is easy."

"Isn't that the truth," she muttered, "but I'm here now. So hopefully you can do your worst, and it won't be half as bad as what I've already been through recently."

"Hey," he protested. "Surely it can't be that bad to see me."

She smiled at him. "It's not that bad, but it's not that great either."

He nodded. "Let's hope we can get you back on your feet pretty fast," he began. "I'm waiting on the updated medical records, since they didn't come with you."

"Not surprised," she noted, yawning.

He frowned at her and asked, "You need food?" He

looked over at the muffin on her bedside table. "Or did somebody bring you something?"

"That's from Dennis earlier this morning."

"Good. You two all okay?"

She smiled at him and nodded. "It's all okay. With Dennis, everything's always okay."

"He hurts and bleeds like every other man," Shane shared. "He just doesn't show it."

She stopped, startled. Then she sighed. "That's a very good point. I didn't mean to belittle him in any way."

"I hear that," Shane replied. "You want to tell me where your major problems are today?"

"The leg and the hip," she pointed out. "I did get a hip replacement, where they found bone spurs and scraped those off the pelvic girdle," she explained, her words rushed, trying to tell him all she'd been through. "My priority is making sure I'm back up on my feet and strong again."

"Got it."

"It's everything to me," she whispered, "that whole independence thing again."

He nodded. "And what if you can't?"

"Then I won't be terribly happy," she muttered. "However, if that's all I get for a choice, it doesn't really matter, does it?"

"We'll do everything we can to get you back in form," he stated. "We also know that sometimes things don't go quite the way that you want them to."

"Is that a warning?" she asked, staring at him.

"No, I just want to ensure your expectations are reasonable."

She sighed again. "You always were big on that."

"Until I see those records, I don't want you to do all this

work with an idea that you'll walk away scot-free," he clarified, "because you and I both know that won't happen in every situation."

"No, you're right," she confirmed, "and I also admit that I wasn't the best at maintaining all those exercises you sent me home with."

"What?" he asked in mock horror.

She smiled. "As if you haven't heard that a time or two."

"No, not at all," he quipped, with an eye roll. "Everybody starts with the best of intentions, and that momentum goes downhill very quickly when living a life."

"I did have the best of intentions," she noted. "Yet I didn't realize just how quickly life gets in the way."

"And that's what life's all about," he said, with a smile. "It's about challenges. It's about striving to do more and to be better, and very quickly some of what you started out doing ends up going by the wayside because there's just no time for it."

She nodded. "That feels about right," she agreed. "And it's sad because we need more hours in life, but, by the time you work and clean and cook and take care of everything else that has to be done, it just seems as if nothing is left."

"And because nothing is left, what goes first is your health," he noted, with a nod. "But you're back, and this is a refresher course."

She smiled. "And a part of me says I don't deserve it."

He frowned at that. "Why on earth not?"

She shrugged. "I guess I feel, if I had done my exercises routinely, my reflexes would have been faster, better, stronger. So I could have sidestepped that car, and I wouldn't have been wiped out quite so badly."

"Wow," he murmured. "That's a lot of guilt to carry on

your shoulders." She stared at him, but he shrugged. "Life happens. Maybe your reflexes weren't as good as you think they should be, but maybe they're better than what so many other people's are. Maybe if it had been anybody else, they might've died from that accident," he suggested. "So why don't we park the guilt and do our best to just see how far we can bring you? Barring any surprises in your latest medical records, nothing you've mentioned here sounds terrible. It all is quite doable, and, for that, I'm very grateful because it could have been so much worse."

"Really?" she asked, staring at him hopefully.

"Absolutely. Obviously I'm not minimizing what's going on in your body," he clarified, "but we can fix an awful lot of things in our rehab program."

"I'm glad to hear that," she replied, bolstered for once.

"Are you ambulatory?"

"Some, not really," she replied, "and that's one of the problems. Of course, right after the hip surgery, they made me get up and down all the time."

"Sure, blood clots form, and all kinds of other medical headaches happen," he noted. "Yet you came in here not on a gurney but under your own power. What was that about?"

"Stubbornness. Plus, I can't sit for very long," she shared. "So it's either lie down, or get up and down all the time."

"Right." Shane nodded. "Let's see if we can get a wheelchair and get you up and at least down for breakfast."

She waited until he came back with a wheelchair for her. "I am ambulatory in the sense that I can get to the bathroom," she added. "I had a walker, and that helped sometimes. Of course my prosthetic was damaged in the accident, so the one I have is temporary and doesn't fit well."

"Don't worry about it," Shane noted. "We'll start this way in the wheelchair and take a look and just see how many problems you might have trying to do what you need to do, and we'll go from there."

Feeling a little bit better after their talk, Shane got her into the wheelchair and then pushed her to the dining room. "I can push myself," she stated.

"I'm sure you can, and, even if you can't, you'll power through to prove that you can, right?"

"Ouch," she muttered.

"Hey, I haven't forgotten how stubbornly independent you are," he declared. "I'm not trying to push your buttons either. I'm just not sure how much of this is at the same level of importance as it was to you before."

"Wow, I made quite an impression back then, didn't I?" And even saying that was hard because she had been very strict about being independent.

"Not everybody can be independent all the time," Shane pointed out, "and everybody needs some help some of the time."

"Right," she murmured. "Let's hope that we can find a middle ground." He chuckled at that, and, as they neared the dining room, the noise surprised her. "Well," she said, "some things you never forget."

"What's that?" he asked.

"The noise for one. Coming in here at mealtimes, the din always bothered me."

"A din," he repeated. "The actual noise? Does it bother your ears?"

"I never really made a big thing out of it," she replied, "but it was one of the reasons I would skedaddle on back to my room as much as I did." He frowned at her, but she shrugged. "It wasn't anything worth talking about."

"Says you," he countered. "Those things make a difference to us."

"Maybe, but it's not as if all that noise could change, not just for me."

"Maybe not, maybe it's low on your priority list right now. However, you do realize that your hearing and your balance are linked, right? Regardless, that hearing sensitivity you have isn't something you just have to live with, and it doesn't mean we couldn't do something to minimize it."

She shrugged. "It doesn't matter." She was more disturbed right now to feel the fatigue hitting her again, just from sitting upright in a wheelchair. She shifted uneasily in the chair.

"How long can you handle sitting?" Shane asked.

"Half an hour to forty-five minutes," she shared. "Other than that I've got to get up and move around or lie down."

"Good enough. So you'll make it through breakfast?"

"I'll make it through breakfast," she confirmed, with a nod. As she got into the dining room, Dennis stared directly at her. She sucked in her breath.

Shane placed his hand gently on her shoulder and asked her again, from a different perspective, "Will you make it through breakfast?"

She let out a long, slow breath. "Yes, at least, I think so." She looked back up at him and frowned. "Some days are easier than others."

"Yeah, and, once you get used to being around Dennis again, you'll be fine. However, after today? The two of you need to work it out."

"And if there's nothing to work out?"

"Then you won't have to worry about it, will you?" he

teased, with a chuckle. "Besides, there are good and bad things about all this. Maybe this is a good thing."

"Maybe," she conceded, "but it feels as if I hurt him."

He stared down at her. "Maybe then, this is a chance for you to *un*hurt him."

She chuckled at that. "I don't even know why I'm laughing, because really, this is not funny."

"It's not funny," Shane agreed, "but it is life. And right now it's facing you. So it's up to you as to how you want to go forward."

She winced at that. "Everything's not quite so easy or so straightforward."

"No, but with Dennis it usually is."

She stared up at the huge man, busily serving people in line, and nodded. "He's always been very straightforward, hasn't he?"

"That's one word for it, and yet I would not in any way make him out to be so simple."

She chuckled. "Dennis is very complex," she agreed. "A fascinating, frustrating, but incredibly complex man."

"Ah, sounds as if you do know him well."

"As you are well aware," she stated crossly, "I do know him very well."

IT TOOK AWAY Dennis's breath to see her come into his dining room again. He plastered on a smile, although he wanted to race over and give her a big hug and ask if he could do anything to make her day better. However, he already knew that she was as prickly as a cactus five years ago and hadn't changed any. So, if she didn't want help, she by

God didn't want help and don't anybody dare suggest otherwise.

Dennis almost smiled at the memory. And caught sight of her again. They studied each other for a long moment across the huge room. And then Shane spoke to Yvonne, before leaving her to join Dani in a private discussion. Yvonne wheeled slowly forward, getting into line at the buffet, and eventually in front of Dennis.

He nodded to her. "Did you have a good rest?"

"As well as I can expect," she replied.

He had tried to keep his tone neutral, when, of course, he wanted to know everything about her. Still, he also knew that going down that pathway could be incredibly painful. Just because he loved somebody didn't mean that now was the time or the place to discuss it. He'd already been there once before, and her rejection had been devastating—as all of his friends here knew.

She looked down at the food, seeing what was on offer this morning.

He asked, "Do you have an appetite?"

"I do, but my digestive tract isn't doing all that great after my latest accident." He stared at her, but she shrugged and continued. "You would think the original injury would have done enough damage, yet I came through that okay," she shared. "Now, the car accident? I lost a chunk of my liver, and I lost my spleen. On top of that, my gallbladder's got days where it doesn't remember to function."

"Interesting," Dennis murmured. "You're on a special diet then?"

"Definitely need easy-on-the-stomach type foods." She opted for a bowl of scrambled eggs and then a little bit of yogurt and fresh fruit.

He quickly served her what she needed and asked, "Can you take it over on your own?"

"I can," she replied. "I can even walk short distances. However, the problem is walking back to my room. Plus, sitting for very long periods doesn't do me any good." But she accepted the tray with bowls of food and moved her way to the drinks station, grabbing a bottled water. She looked around to see who she could sit with.

Shane and Dani were busy talking at the other end of the dining room, all by themselves. It seemed to be a private discussion. And, of course, Dennis was busy. However, Yvonne heard a startled gasp and turned to see Stan.

He took one look at her and immediately walked over, bent down, and gave her a hug. "When we see people leave, the last thing we want, even though we don't mean it personally, is to see them back here for medical reasons. The grapevine didn't come to my corner and let me know that you were here," he muttered, almost affronted.

She smiled. "It doesn't take long for the news to travel around Hathaway House."

"No, not at all," he agreed. "Hang on while I go grab some food, and I'll sit with you." And, with that, he disappeared.

Yvonne had to admit it was nice to have a friend to join her at mealtimes. As he soon sat down beside her with a plate of bacon and eggs and sausages, she shook her head. "How is it that you never gain any weight?"

"Lots of us who live and work here don't. I figure it's all the running around we do. We are on our feet an awful lot," he suggested. "I mean, look at Dennis. He's still the same size he always has been."

She didn't need to have that pointed out. She'd already

checked him out pretty carefully as soon as she'd seen him. She smiled over at Stan and changed the subject. "How's work?"

"Crazy busy," he replied cheerfully, "but that's a good thing."

"And you still love what you're doing? You're still happy with your decision to be here?"

"Absolutely," he declared. "And you went back to school and became what?" he asked.

"A computer programmer," she stated, with a wry smile. "All the hours killed me. I had a lot to learn, and that was all done in my spare time."

He nodded. "From everything I've heard about going back to school and starting over again, that has to be one of the hardest to get through."

"It is," she agreed, "and it's not something that I can't change. I just need to get into an easier job."

"Right." Stan nodded. "And you're here now because …?" He shook his head. "Is this a relapse?"

"No, the result of a car accident." Whatever he'd been expecting to hear, obviously her response wasn't it.

His jaw dropped, and he stared at her. "Oh, good Lord, no."

She nodded. "I was on the crosswalk when I got hit by a drunk driver."

"Oh my goodness. After everything you've already been through?"

"I know. Life's a bit of a … Life's got a strange sense of humor, doesn't it? I'm here because Dani fit me in."

"That's a good thing," Stan noted.

"I know. I definitely did not want to come back to rehab, or to fail, or to get into an accident, or anything like that." She sighed. "Still, it's great to have as many friends here as I do," she murmured. "But being here as a rehab patient? … It was hard work last time, and a part of me says I'm not up for it this time."

He stared at her in astonishment and then shook his head. "That's not the woman I knew. She was up for everything."

"And she got old and tired and worn down. She spent so much time trying to achieve that she forgot to live."

"Ah," he murmured. "So maybe it's a good thing you're here right now, to give you a chance to regroup, to figure out where you want to go from here, and to choose a new life that's hopefully not quite so crazy."

"Is that possible?" she asked.

"I think so," he stated. "I mean, we all should have some joy in life, outside of just the work that we love."

And, with that, she watched as one of the veterans in a wheelchair moved past her. He was missing an arm and both legs. "Listen to me, complaining. Then I look at so many people here who are worse off than me physically. Even after the car accident, taking a severe hit in so many ways, I'm still way better off than a lot of people here."

She shuddered as she thought about it because she'd come close to losing two limbs, but Shane had determined that she should keep the one leg that had caused her a lot of trouble and the arm that had refused to cooperate for a long time. Now they both functioned decently.

"And so you are dealing with the same injuries again?" Stan asked.

"No, and I should be very grateful for that because the recent set of surgeons didn't quite understand why those body parts hadn't been affected. Yet I'm sure Shane would say it's because of all the rehab work that we did ahead of time, which was why those parts of my body were doing as well as they were." Yvonne shrugged. "Now it's basically my lower back and hips."

"And that is really no surprise," Stan noted. "Whenever car accidents are involved, the back and hips seem to always be affected." Stan shook his head. "And some of those injuries can be absolutely brutal."

She smiled. "Some of them? I'm hoping Shane can pull another miracle out of a hat."

"Well, if anybody can," Stan declared cheerfully, "you know it'll be Shane. At least you're not bothered about being here."

"I was, for all of five minutes," she shared, with a laugh. "Then I very quickly realized all the benefits that I had the first time around, and I'm still hoping I'll get those this second time around." She watched as Stan polished off his breakfast. "And, besides," she added in a teasing tone, "it's really nice to have a chance to reconnect with friends."

He raised his eyebrows. "We were always here," he pointed out.

"I know, but, after I left"—her gaze drifted to Dennis— "it felt as if I needed to *leave*-leave."

"But you didn't have to cut all ties," Stan argued, "not in any way. That was always just your perception."

"And yet when it is a perception," she countered, "I took it that way, right or wrong, and it's very hard to come back from that."

"And yet now you're here," Stan noted cheerfully. "So that part's already taken care of."

She smiled at him, happy to see him accept her uncondi-tionally. She shook her head at herself. *Just another character flaw that I need to work on.*

Stan gathered his dishes again on his tray. "I've got to get back to work. I've got a busy day. You know the drill. Come down anytime you want. We're more than happy to see you, and so are the animals." And, with that, he hopped up and took off.

She sat here with the rest of her meal, wishing she'd picked up a coffee to sit and enjoy afterward, but it was over on the far side, and a lot of people were around that drinks station. So she would wait for that area to clear a bit. It was foolish to be so hyperaware of every movement that Dennis made, but that's just the way it was for Yvonne. It had been the way of it before too. She would come inside the dining room, and all her senses would immediately come alive. She knew the chance of ever finding anybody like Dennis was almost nonexistent. Of course people say there are doubles and doppelgangers all over the world, but Dennis was a special soul.

And she'd hurt him dreadfully.

She could forgive herself for a lot of things in life, but hurting Dennis would be one that she struggled with until the day she died. She also needed to forgive herself because, well, if she'd had any brains in her head, she never would have left him behind. He wanted her to stay close, but she didn't have it in her. She had ambition. She had plans. She would be somebody. The accident—the original one—had only spurred her on to being more and more of what she thought she wanted to be.

Instead she had been a fool, and she'd walked away from everything that counted.

Chapter 3

TWO DAYS LATER Dennis seemed to always have his radar on Yvonne, on her every move, on everybody who stopped to say hi to her, on every person who came close to her vicinity. Dennis didn't know why he was still so hyper-aware of her, and God knows Dennis would be better off if he wasn't. Yet she'd been an important part of his life at one point in time, and it was hard to even imagine that she was back here now. He had to think he was being offered a second chance with her, but then his brain would tell him to wait and see on that angle. Regardless, he kept checking on her to ensure that he wasn't fooling himself, that she was truly here again.

For good or for bad, as it dealt with him.

He sighed, resigned to stay back, waiting for permission from Yvonne to get closer.

When he realized that she'd finished eating, and her usual mealtime companion Stan had left, Dennis quickly poured a cup of coffee and brought it over for her. Not taking care of her was something so foreign to him that it wasn't anything he could stop. Not until she told him to butt out. And that would come, just because that's who she was. However, in the meantime, if he could do something to make her transition back to Hathaway House a little bit easier, then he was all for it.

Dennis placed the cup in front of her. "I don't know if you still take it the same way."

Yvonne eyed the cup and then nodded at him. "Yes, black." She smiled. "How can you always be so nice?"

"Being nice doesn't come with an expiration date," he noted, studying her. "Sometimes it just requires opening yourself up a little more."

"I don't know about that," she countered. "You're the only person I know who's always this nice."

He chuckled. "In that case, you need to widen the group of people who you know."

"You could be right," she admitted. "I've been working with big corporations in high-pressure jobs. It's definitely not a great environment. Everyone is stressed to the max. Even if they are nice, the situation doesn't let them show it."

"No, I can't imagine what you do. I thought you would go into law, where you were helping women."

"I did too," she noted glumly. "Didn't work out that way."

"It's not as if it's a done deal where you can't pursue it. You've got lots of time where you can switch careers, if you want to."

"Are you still happy here?" she asked.

He nodded. "Yep."

"Still happy doing the same thing?" she asked, motioning at the rag in his hand.

He looked down at it, smiled, and replied, "This is just one of those mundane parts of my work. It never defined me."

"No, it never did before either," she agreed. "You're one of the few men I know who was totally okay to wait on people and to clean tables and chairs and to not feel diminished by it."

"That is an interesting statement. I can't say I ever felt diminished by anything I did, not when I was of service to someone. Some people are meant to be of service, and some people, well, I guess they're not."

"I don't hear that phrase often," she noted. "Matter of fact I don't think I've ever heard somebody say that they've been in a service industry—unless it's military service."

"That's never been the usual, as you well know," he pointed out. "However, I always felt as if what I was doing was still important."

"And it is," she stated. "Some of us are just a little slow to get it." She tossed back the rest of her coffee, handed him her cup, and said, "I guess I need to go get prepped."

"Prepped for what?"

She winced. "Shane."

Dennis burst out laughing. "He knows so much more about the latest rehab tricks and tips and techniques now too," he shared. "Yet he's still not anybody to be scared of."

"Ha," she muttered. "That's because you're on that side of the table, not on this one."

Dennis walked around to stand beside her. "Still looks as if Shane's a normal guy to me."

She rolled her eyes and half chuckled. "Anyway, I need to go." She smiled at him. "Thanks."

"For what?" he asked. "I just brought you a cup of coffee."

She nodded. "For being you." And, with yet another cryptic comment, she slowly wheeled herself from the dining room.

BACK IN HER room Yvonne changed into a looser T-shirt, one that gave her a little bit more room for movement, and slowly wheeled her way to Shane, who was waiting for her.

He looked up and smiled. "Hey. How did you do at breakfast?"

"I didn't do too badly. I was there about thirty minutes." She motioned at the mat. "Any chance I can get out of the chair?"

He nodded. "Absolutely. Floor or standing?"

"Depends on what you've got planned," she replied. "Floor's probably easier, if we'll be a while."

"Down to the floor it is then," he agreed.

She made her way to her knees and slowly lowered herself to the floor. She rolled over until she was on her back, and a sigh of relief slipped out.

"It really does help, *huh*?" Shane asked.

"It really does help," she murmured. "So many things hurt these days."

"Well, you're still fresh from that car accident and the surgery thereafter," he pointed out.

"I know, and I'm not sure I have the strength to fight that good fight anymore."

He shrugged. "I remember back when, one of the things that we tried to get through to you was how some things you needed to fight and other things you needed to just relax about," he shared. "Maybe this time you'll take a little more relaxed pathway to rehab."

She rolled her head and frowned at him.

He laughed. "Or maybe not."

"I never got that technique down pat," she admitted. She rubbed her hands over her arms, as a chill passed over her.

"Are you cold?" Shane asked in concern.

"Not necessarily cold," she clarified. "Sometimes you look back on your life, and you wonder at the choices you made—considering why and how you could possibly have made the decisions you did—and then question how you're supposed to go back and make better choices. You know what I mean?"

"Kind of," he hedged, with a cautious note in his tone.

She frowned at him. "Of course not. You don't have a clue what I'm talking about."

"I think we've all made choices that we've regretted," he shared, "but you're among friends here. So any choice that you want to revisit, it's available to you."

"Maybe," she murmured. And then she yawned a big, long jaw-breaking yawn.

"Still tired?"

"Yes," she murmured. "Still tired *still*. Yet it's more than just tired. It's a bone-weary fatigue."

"I guess you've been working too hard lately, haven't you?"

"I've been working too hard since I left Hathaway House the last time," she admitted. "And I've never really had a chance to stop and to take a break."

"Which is also likely why you're so exhausted right now," he noted. "I think, for today especially, you need to just head back to your room and rest."

"I don't know about that," she argued. "I need to get whatever benefit I can get, while I can."

"And yet you're not ready," he declared, "not ready at all."

She winced and stared at him. "But you could help me get ready."

"Nope, you wore yourself to the bone the last time with all that go-getter high-energy *determined to set the world on fire* mentality," he shared. "What I see right now is a completely different person."

"But she's getting me immediately sent back to my room. She needs to take a back seat in my life."

He stared at her for a long moment. "Maybe you should start with some shrink sessions."

She snorted. "Do I have to?"

"Yeah," he said, making a quick decision. "I think you do."

"I don't want to have anything to do with that, if I have a choice."

"If you're here, counseling is part of it," he told her. "Since I have no medicals still on your recent events, I have no idea yet how bad these new injuries are, how much the surgery helped. Thus, I don't know what progress we'll make without those records. And you should be happy and grateful in dealing and living with whatever point we can get you back to."

"I already came to terms with that," she muttered.

"But did you?" he asked. "Because you left here last time, bound and determined that nothing would hold you back. I'm not seeing that this time."

"No." She sighed. "I think that's because I am so very tired. It's hard to always find that *oomph* to get up and go when you don't want to anymore, when you're afraid that everything that you've already done is for nought. That explains why I am here, right back at the same place again."

"You're hardly back to the same place physically and mentally," he pointed out, with an odd look in her direction.

"Maybe, but it does feel as if I've come full circle."

"Then maybe you should look at the last time you were here as a practice run."

She stared at him. "That was not much of a practice run," she declared immediately.

He laughed. "Okay, so maybe that's not the best way to look at it. However, you already did this once, so you know how much you can achieve."

"I also know what I lost," she admitted. "And I also know what that cost me."

"And I presume those statements have absolutely nothing to do with the rehab work we're talking about right now. Instead it seems to have everything to do with Dennis."

She stared at him for a moment. "I guess it's pretty obvious, isn't it?"

"You guys were pretty intense back then, and then you left."

"And I learned my lesson, or at least one," she corrected. "I wish I'd had the guts to understand what I needed to do back then, instead of always pushing, pushing, pushing."

"If that's what you did back then," Shane began, "maybe that's what you needed to do. You can't go back and change the past. … All you can do is make peace with it and move forward."

"And that's the problem I'm struggling with," she stated, "and I don't know if this accident hadn't happened would I have always just held that inside and not done anything about it?"

"If that is the case, then I'm really glad you're here. If nothing else, it'll give you a chance to clear your history and to start fresh again," Shane explained. "You can't keep dragging that stuff around in your head, in your heart, and in your soul. All that emotional baggage and judgment weighs you down, and it stops you from being the best that you can be." He shook his head. "So doctor's orders. Head back to bed and stay there, for the rest of the day." And, with that, he packed up his stuff and walked out.

IT WAS HARD for Dennis to ignore Yvonne. But, as her first few days went by, and he saw her settling in somewhat—although she looked incredibly tired—he relaxed. And, as he relaxed, everybody around him relaxed.

Ilse came up to him and said, "Good, we made it through the first few days of Yvonne's return, so maybe you'll be okay now." He looked over at her in surprise. She nodded. "Believe me that everybody's noticed."

"Of course they have," he muttered, with a wince. "Can't say I like being on public display."

"And yet so many of us have already been through it," she noted.

"And so have I, once before," he murmured, giving her a pointed look.

"That doesn't mean that this time will be the same."

"No, but that doesn't mean that it would be anything different. I have no reason to go in that direction anymore," he muttered. "I can only open up myself to just so much pain."

"Nope," she argued, "you're wrong there. You will continue to open yourself up because you love, and when you love and where you love is very deep," she pointed out. "You care about people, even when they don't necessarily have the wherewithal to care about anybody else but themselves."

He immediately frowned.

Ilse added, "I'm not saying that about Yvonne specifically. I'm not insulting her in any way. However, you will always be the first one to offer the shirt off your back, even if so many of us don't agree with it."

He stared at her.

Ilse shrugged. "I like Yvonne just fine, but she hurt you. So, from my point of view, I'll move forward ever-so-slightly now, just to see how things will be this time."

"For all I know, she's married," he grumbled, looking at Ilse intently. "I don't know anything about who she is right now. It's been years."

"Five," Ilse noted. "It's been five years. And, in those five years, she's gone through a lot, but that doesn't mean that I'm necessarily ready to welcome her with open arms."

He smiled. "And yet you say that, and then I see you out there doing what you can to make her comfortable and to find out what are her favorite dishes."

Ilse's lips quirked. "And here I thought that was more about you."

He shrugged. "You're right. Still, I shouldn't be focusing on her so much. We have a lot of other patients here now. Honestly, Hathaway's gotten so big that I'm scared it'll be in danger of getting too big."

"I already talked to Dani about that because it's a concern that several of us have. Something is very special about what we have right now, and we don't want to lose that special personal touch by getting so massive. And Dani's aware of it. At the same time, she also knows so many people out there need our help."

"And that's the crux of it, isn't it?" Dennis asked. "With so many people in need, how can we not help more?"

"Which is why we got the extra wing and the extra staff,

and-and-and," she replied. "It never really ends."

"Is it too much, do you think?"

"No, I don't think it is, particularly if we keep in mind what makes us special is the people on staff, the extra things that we do, everything that we live with and deal with," Ilse noted. "So, if we keep all that in mind, we won't be in trouble, but it is something I think we need to be judicious about."

"And does Dani agree with you?"

"I don't know." Then Ilse laughed. "Dani has got so much going on with her upcoming wedding that I am not sure she even has the time to think about anything else."

"It is coming fast, isn't it?" Dennis noted. "What, eight weeks, ten weeks?"

"I think it's ten now," Ilse replied. "And then they're off on a honeymoon, for which I'm very grateful because otherwise she would never take a holiday."

"Yeah, she's as much of a workaholic as you are," he teased.

"Look who's talking," she quipped. "Look who's here almost every day of the week."

"Well, Sunday is pretty well self-serve," he noted, "at least for those people who can handle it."

"Exactly, but I still often see you here, helping those you can."

"I'm just being me."

"And I get that, and I respect that. At some point you also should have a life out there too."

"And I have one," he protested. "I'm really happy here. And, no, I'm not hiding away in Hathaway House. I'm not, no matter whatever garbage people say about how I could leave and do so much better elsewhere."

"I would hope that's not what they're saying, but, people being people, probably some do say that."

He nodded. "The bottom line is, I much prefer to be here than a lot of places in life."

"And we're all grateful," she murmured. "You don't get paid enough for a lot of the stuff that you deal with here though."

"No, but it's not as if I'm here for the money either," he noted, with a laugh. "Besides, I have zero expenses. It's pretty easy to have a decent life at Hathaway when you don't have to pay for everything."

"I know." Ilse smiled. "I'm in the same boat. Free food and board. Part of my salary."

"Until you get married."

She flushed. "And honestly, I'm not sure I'm leaving afterward either. Dani is wondering about expanding some of the housing to allow for family quarters."

Dennis raised his eyebrows and nodded. "That's an awesome idea."

Ilse nodded. "And Dani told me that Yvonne never married."

Chapter 4

A WEEK LATER Yvonne stared at the X-rays that Shane had up on the wall, courtesy of the recent sharing of her current medical records. "Wow, they look really bad."

"The one thing that bothers me," he noted, "is that piece of shrapnel that they never removed has shifted."

She looked at where he was pointing and nodded. "I know. They did mention that."

"And they still weren't willing to take it out?"

"They told me that it was better to leave it as it was," she murmured.

Shane shook his head. "I'm not a doctor, but that really worries me. If anything happens while we're working on you, trying to get you back up to strength, what's likely to stop you is *that* very piece of shrapnel."

She felt her heart sinking, as she studied the X-rays. It did look as if it was awfully close to something vital. "What is that?"

"Your liver," he stated calmly. "And that shrapnel wasn't there before." He went through her files and brought up the old X-ray and pointed to where that piece had been sitting way too close to her spine before. "The shrapnel has broken into two pieces, so you have one shard still by your spine and that other part now near your liver."

"Good God," she murmured.

"Right? I'm surprised they didn't bring it up with you."

She frowned, shaking her head. "They mentioned something about shrapnel, but they still didn't advise surgery. Thus, I didn't really think much about it. However, when I see the two X-rays up there side by side, it becomes real to me, more black-and-white." She didn't even know what to say.

"We'll do our best to get you back as strong as we can," Shane stated. "That shrapnel is definitely something to keep an eye on, though."

"Sure," she agreed, "but, short of some catastrophic event, they won't do anything."

"Maybe not. I will talk to the doctors here about your case, though."

She wasn't sure what that meant, but it was a little bit beyond her willingness to study those medical records and to realize all that damage that had been done to her. "The car wreck in some ways helped, and in other ways it seemed to just compound my problems."

"Yes, it helped in some ways in that it realigned some of the bones that we couldn't move before. In a way we're starting right back at square one," he murmured. "These most recent injuries are fresh. They're new. They're different. I don't see anything stopping us from getting you back on your feet as solid as you were before, though. As a matter of fact, these injuries in some ways are less than your original ones."

"Less, but?"

He nodded. "*Less, but* is right. Every injury is something new that we must work with," he shared. "So everything that's gone on before, we can pretty well take off our plate and ignore because this is all a new beginning in terms of rehabbing these current injuries," he shared. "I've worked up a plan that we'll start with, but not today. I just want you to rest, to get your strength back up for another day or so. And then we'll get started." He added, "I need another day to work some extra things into your plan."

He kept studying the X-rays, whereas she was already past it. If she spent all her time thinking about the damage that that car accident had done, or what damage those two pieces of shrapnel could still do if they shifted, well, there just wasn't any living at all with her fears. She announced, "In that case, I'll head to lunch."

He smiled at her and nodded. "You do that." As she got to the door, he asked, "How are you and Dennis making out?"

"Fine," she replied, without stopping her exit, not giving him a chance to ask anything further.

She headed out to the dining room. Her mind was still preoccupied with her X-rays. It looked bad when she looked at them closely. But now that she had seen all that damage to her body, past and present, she realized that her latest damage was piled on top of her previous damage and that her new scar tissue was there along with her old scar tissue.

To her, it looked to be a monumental rehab job. She trusted Shane to get her as good as she could be, but it seemed now that *as good as it could be* just wouldn't be very good at all.

Depressed, not sure what she should've done instead of heading to the dining room, she got in line at the buffet counter, using her wheelchair with an adroitness that she hadn't expected and didn't want to have. But after several months back in a wheelchair, both before and after her hip surgery, it was what it was. As she got up to the front of the line, there was Dennis.

He frowned at her. "You look tired today."

She nodded. "Yeah, I am a bit."

"What can I get you?"

She quickly made her selection, and, when he handed her the plate of food, she murmured her thanks and headed to the table in the farthest corner. She didn't feel like being social. She didn't feel like being even halfway friendly to anybody. It was just that kind of a day, where she wanted to shut herself away and try to ignore everybody and everything. But the world wouldn't cooperate.

Almost as soon as she sat down, her table filled up around her, and she was surprised because it used to not be quite so full here at Hathaway House. Maybe that's what it was like these days. She looked around to see that most of the tables were filling up at the same time. Even if she wanted to be antisocial, it would be hard. Another woman sitting beside her chatted away.

She asked Yvonne, "Hey, did you just get here?"

She nodded. "More or less." It was such an odd thing to say that the woman gave her an inquiring look. Yvonne added, "I had a recent car accident, but I was here years ago, getting over a roadside bomb," she murmured. "And now, here I am back again, after getting hit by a drunk driver."

The other woman stared at her in shock.

Yvonne waved her hand. "Don't worry about it. I shouldn't have brought it up."

"Of course you should have," she replied. "In one way or another we're all in the same boat here. Obviously everybody's issues are different, but we all need to heal."

"Are you a patient here?" Yvonne eyed the woman, but she appeared to be healthy. "How long have you been here?"

she asked.

"I'm just about done now," she replied, with a smile. "Shane's putting the final touches on some of my exercises. I'm leaving on Friday."

"Wow, I'm envious."

"I'm also getting married in two weeks." She laughed elatedly. "So that just adds to it."

"Good for you," Yvonne replied.

"I didn't want to get married until I could walk down the aisle. And then he had a close call on an accident himself just a few weeks back," she murmured. "And I realized how foolish it was. We set all these goals, about how we won't do this until that happens, and it's ridiculous. His accident helped me to see that I just wanted to get married and to spend whatever time I have with him because we have no guarantee that we'll get that time just because we think we will." And, with that, the woman quickly finished off her parfait and said goodbye and disappeared.

Yet her words had a lasting effect on Yvonne because they mirrored a lot of what she had been thinking for the last little while. She'd done everything she could to get on her feet and to get out of here last time. And now she was right back at square one, and it felt as if she'd done everything for nought. Matter of fact, it felt as if she'd made it even worse. When somebody sat down beside her, she looked up to see Dani. Her smile was bright and natural. Yvonne smiled back. "You guys got busier."

"We got bigger," Dani noted, with a nod. "Sometimes I wonder if it was the right thing to do."

"As long as you can maintain that love and affection that everybody here seems to have for each other," Yvonne replied, "I think it's fine, as that is what makes you guys so special."

Dani looked at her in surprise and then laughed. "That is interesting to hear," she murmured. "And we are trying to keep a lot of what we have the same, but, of course, as you get bigger, you have to adjust."

"How's Ilse doing with the extra food load?"

"She's got more staff to help her now too," Dani shared. "So she's doing great."

"And I hear you're getting married."

"I am, indeed." Dani flushed. "I can't wait. Seems like forever."

"And he's a vet?" she asked. "Going to be a veterinarian?"

"Wow, the rumor mill's really been working overtime."

"Of course it has," Yvonne noted, with a smile. "Plus, everybody's trying to catch me up on the news."

"Of course. Yes, Aaron will soon start working with Stan downstairs. We've been maintaining our relationship long distance, and that's been really tough," Dani admitted. "He's done with school now, coming back here, working with Stan in a couple weeks, at least I hope it's a couple weeks. Aaron still has a few exams to finish off, and then we'll get married."

"I'm really happy for you," Yvonne said. "You deserve it."

At that, Dani smiled at her. "Thank you. You deserve happiness too, you know?"

It was such an odd thing for her to say that Yvonne frowned at her and asked, "Do I act or speak or whatever as if I don't deserve happiness?" she asked.

"No, I think in your heart of hearts you think you made a mistake, and you don't know how to go back."

"Ouch. I forgot how absolutely intuitive and spot-on everybody here is."

Dani laughed. "I don't know about any of us being intuitive and spot-on," she began, "but I can tell you that we all come from the heart, and we know when somebody is hurting."

"I guess my leaving was hard on him last time, wasn't it?"

"Yep, it sure was. Let's just take the word *hard* out of it and put *devastating* in there."

She winced at that. "Lord, I was such a fool."

"Nope, you weren't, and you had to do what you thought was right back then."

"Even if it was so obviously wrong?"

"I don't know that there was anything that was so obviously wrong about anything. Sometimes we don't know if it's wrong unless we try it first. Would you rather regret what you did or instead regret what you failed to do?" Dani asked, not expecting an answer. "Life happens, whether we like it or not. It's just not always easy to find the right answer out there. While we try hard, that doesn't give us any guarantees that what we do will be the correct choice for us. You should go with your gut, choosing the best decision that you have ahead of you at the time. You did that. Don't regret doing it. I would be more inclined to think you might regret *not* doing it. If you change that decision now, that's another option you have."

"I'm not sure it is available anymore," Yvonne noted, her gaze straying to where Dennis was talking with other people. "It doesn't seem to matter to him whether I'm here or not."

"That's not true," Dani countered. "It matters. He's also hurting over the fact that you're hurting. He doesn't want to see that, but he also probably doesn't know what to do about it."

"Nothing he can do," Yvonne muttered. "That's the thing. It will be up to me again."

"Well, last time it had to be you all alone because you set it up that way," Dani pointed out in a very gentle tone. "Maybe this time you can learn to accept help, learn to accept support, learn to accept that other people can be at your side, can be part of your journey and won't judge you for your choices," Dani explained. "You were always afraid that you weren't doing enough, that you had to do so much more. … I'm not sure that that was true."

"Maybe not," she murmured. "But it sure seemed as if there just wasn't a whole lotta choice."

"And I get that," Dani replied. "In your mind there was no choice because you were on a path. You were determined to go off and to do all these things. And he let you go, without any argument."

"And maybe that wasn't good either," Yvonne muttered, staring at the man who had captured her heart so long ago, a man who she now couldn't even bear to talk to, just confirming her fears that he didn't want anything to do with her.

"I'm not sure about that," Dani countered. "I think loving and letting go is a very important lesson. If that person comes back to you, then you're both truly blessed. But if not? … If they don't belong together, then it wasn't meant to be," Dani stated, her words spoken low and very calmly.

At that, Yvonne had to smile. "I forgot what a cheerleader you are."

"Hey, it goes with the territory," she murmured. "Even if it's not so much cheerleading as just trying to be supportive."

"Right, but there's support, and then there's support."

"No, there's just plain support. So, if you need anything, you let me know. If you need to see a surgeon or another doctor, then you let me know that as well," she added. "I think you're supposed to see your specialist next … week?"

"Yes, I wanted to see what we can do here first."

"Got it."

DENNIS WATCHED YVONNE over the next few days, but she didn't seem to be any happier or any stronger. Instead she appeared somewhat defeated, as if the return to rehab was harder than she expected. Finally at the end of dinner one night, when she was sitting alone out on the deck, he came out with a cup of coffee and sat down beside her. "Hey. How are you adapting?"

She looked over at him cautiously, as if expecting him to blow up at her or something.

It almost broke his heart. Yes, he'd been devastated when she left, but it had also been her choice, and he was an adult. And life? Well, life just sometimes wasn't what you wanted it to be.

She shrugged. "It's not easy being back. I hadn't even considered returning until they called me about a job interview, and I turned it into a patient interview."

"Sounds as if the call was perfect timing," he noted, "and I gather the injuries are different this time."

She nodded. "Yeah, the car accident seems to have added to some of my other problems."

He was sorry about that, but it made sense. You couldn't

expect to walk away from a car accident after having had as much surgery and recovery as she had had beforehand and expect it to be as good as gold. "At least you're in the right place," he said gently.

She nodded. "That's my hope at least," she murmured. "Unfortunately—"

"Unfortunately what?" he asked curiously.

"The shrapnel has moved," she replied. "Well, the shrapnel has broken into two pieces, and both pieces are moving."

"So can they remove it now?"

"They didn't mention it before," she shared. "I'm supposed to see the specialist soon. It was set for next month, but Shane wants them to take a look at it earlier."

"If Shane wants you to, then you should," Dennis stated.

"Shane talked to the doctors," she shared. "Shane's the one who started everything going down that pathway, and now they want me to go see my specialist early."

"Then it's a good thing. Shane only wants what's best for you."

"I know, but the thought of the surgeon going in after that shrapnel?" She winced. "It doesn't sound good to me."

"But if it's moved and if it's accessible for them to get it out safely now, I think that would be easier for you."

"Maybe," she murmured, "but, of course, waiting to see him is nerve-racking."

He nodded. "How will you get there?"

"I think somebody from here is taking me," she shared, "but honestly, I didn't ask Dani that."

"We have transports for things like that," Dennis stated, with a nod. "So I'm sure somebody will handle it." They didn't say anything for a long moment, and he wasn't sure just what to say. Finally he got up. "I need to get back to work."

At that, she nodded and smiled. "Thanks for stopping by."

He didn't know what to say, so he spoke from the heart. "Always for you." And, with that, he left. As he got back into the kitchen, the other staff looked over at him. He shrugged. "You can't go backward in time," he murmured.

He knew they wouldn't necessarily understand, but he understood. Things had changed. She'd changed. He'd changed. He didn't know if they still had anything or not, but, if she wasn't willing to go in that direction again, he couldn't change those circumstances. It was heartbreaking to see her as despondent as she was, but that shrapnel was still an ongoing concern. From his perspective it was a good time to deal with it.

Each day he kept an eye on her, seeing the physical and emotional pain that she was in, trying to help from a distance, yet knowing that he couldn't do anything if she didn't let him in. As long as she was letting somebody in, that was fine. He saw her a lot with Shane, with Stan, and with Dani, but that seemed to be the end of her interactions among people in Hathaway House.

When he caught her moving very slowly at breakfast early one morning, he said, "Today would be a good day for you to stay in bed."

She stared at him and nodded. "Wouldn't that be nice?"

"If you need it, you should take it," Dennis suggested, trying hard not to have that demanding tone in his voice. They'd gone through this several times when she'd been here before, where he wanted her to take it easy, but she'd been driven to do so much more than she should have. But she'd been stronger than all of them knew, and she'd been right, and he'd been wrong. She'd put all that hard work to good use and had gotten out of here in good timing.

She added, "I go in to see the specialist today."

He frowned. "Oh. So do you want breakfast?"

She stared at him and shook her head. "No, I'm not sure how I'll find the trip."

"Is that coming from your back?" She nodded. "Has that got anything to do with the shrapnel?" Dennis asked.

She sighed. "Both, plus just sitting still for too long." And, with that, she took her cup of coffee and headed out on the deck.

When Shane showed up, Dennis asked him, "Is all that extra pain that she's in coming from the shrapnel?"

"That's one of the reasons I wanted her to see her surgeon," Shane replied in a very low voice. "I'm not exactly sure, but I think it's time to get it out."

Dennis winced at that. "I know she's been really terrified about that for a long time."

"Yeah, and this added surgery won't be any easier on her either," Shane pointed out. "Nothing I can do for her until we deal with some of these underlying issues." Not a whole lot else Shane could say. And he had to stay as confidential as he could over all this.

Yet it's not as if Dennis wasn't in the know. He just wasn't in Yvonne's inner circle this time around. And to recognize that was even harder to accept. He had no right to be there either. He watched from a distance as Yvonne got ready to leave, and then, even after the transport vehicle had left, he went out to the front lobby to check with Dani that they had got off okay.

"Yes, they did. She won't be home until lunchtime."

He nodded. "I've got lots to keep me busy until then."

"Has she talked to you at all?"

"Not very much. Feels as if she's keeping me an arm's distance away."

At that, Dani nodded. "I would be surprised if she *wasn't* doing that."

"Yet she's a different person entirely," Dennis shared. "This version's more beaten. More … I don't know how to explain it. Seems she took a licking from life, and it's got the better of her this time."

"And in some ways that might be true," Dani agreed, "but don't give up on her. She's a fighter. We need to figure out what's happening with that shrapnel."

"I can't believe they allowed her to travel as it is. Maybe it moved during the trip here."

"Maybe. The concern is whether it's *still* moving, in which case all her rehab therapy must come to an immediate stop, while they decide what to do."

"She won't like that much."

"No, she won't, but she's holding back a lot of the pain, I think," Dani suggested. "That's something else we'll have to talk to her about when she returns."

He nodded. "She never did like taking painkillers. They make her sick to her stomach."

"She may not like the side effects of taking them," Dani noted, with a smile. "However, she should also remember that progress can't happen if she's overwhelmed with pain. Pain itself is debilitating. We need to get her to the point where she's at least managing the pain."

With nothing else to do, and a whole lot on his mind, Dennis headed back to the kitchen to work.

Chapter 5

YVONNE STARED AT her military surgeon and shook her head. "You still don't want to remove them?" she asked in disbelief.

He frowned and shook his head. "You've got two pieces of shrapnel. The original piece in there has broken. You have one jabbing up against your liver and one jabbing up against your spine," he explained. "Taking the piece near the liver might be possible," he muttered, as he studied today's X-rays. "But to go in there and not get both of them won't be an option."

"When would it be an option?" she asked, her voice faint, as she studied the same pictures but now with a new perspective.

"Only under extreme circumstances," the doctor replied. "Unless you're prepared for paralysis."

"I'm in a wheelchair already," she noted, grasping for humor but not finding any.

He nodded. "This is high up your spine. Yet you would still quite likely end up with the full use of your upper body, at least your chest area and your arms," he noted, "but beyond that? I'm not so sure. Something could go wrong, and it could cause bleeding, and we would have a hard time stopping the blood loss."

None of this was what she wanted to hear and was beyond devastating. "So, as far as you're concerned, it'll stay like this?"

"I think we should let it stay as is," he suggested, "providing you don't have any falls and nothing else goes wrong. So no more car accidents. Even then, given some new circumstances, I would like to see it stay where it is."

"And the pain?"

He looked at her and frowned. "Honestly? Painkillers."

By the time she got back to Hathaway House, she was so depressed and upset that she wasn't even in the mood to talk to Shane, who was waiting for her.

He took one look at her expression and muttered, "Not good, *huh*?"

"He doesn't want to touch the shrapnel, which is in two pieces now, just like you told me," she confirmed, with a note of bitterness. "One jabbing the liver and one near the spine. He's afraid I'll end up a paraplegic if he goes in after the one against the spine."

"And what about the one up against the liver?"

"He basically didn't give me an answer on that. I think he's hoping that it'll all go away and won't be his problem."

Shane studied her face intently. "And what do you want to do?"

"I would like to get the shrapnel out," she declared. "I tried to tell him that I'm already in a wheelchair, and, if this is what my life will be like, well, then this is what my life will be like."

"And you know your life doesn't have to be like this, right?"

She stared at Shane. "I don't know that. I can walk, and it is nice, even if I can't walk far," she admitted. "I can still handle all my personal needs, and that's very important to me. To lose that would be difficult."

He nodded. "But it wouldn't be impossible."

She smiled. "No, it wouldn't be impossible. I've certainly seen lots of people here dealing with similar issues, but it wouldn't be easy either."

"Not sure *easy* happens here," Shane pointed out. "This appears to be the camp of *not easy*."

She felt the tears clogging up her throat. She nodded. "I need to rest now."

He stepped away to leave. "His report should be coming through in the morning. I'll look at it then."

She just nodded and didn't say anything. The report wouldn't change anything. As far as her surgeon was concerned, this is what she had to live with, and she should basically be happy with it. Didn't matter that she wasn't happy, didn't matter that she was in constant pain, didn't matter that she had huge problems no matter which way she looked at it. It just all seemed to be a headache that never went away, and she would slowly get more and more confined as that lovely shrapnel either got more established—where her body built up scar tissue—or she would have increasing pain. When she got back to her room, she crashed on her bed, trying to relax her back.

It was hard though. If her back wasn't hurting, another body part was. It just seemed as if one was always at war with the other. She closed her eyes and tried to sleep. But the world seemed to be against her. She had multiple people coming in to check on her, on her blood pressure, on her pain level, on everything else. She wasn't sure if they were just checking on her to ensure she was alive and well and not suicidal—although that thought hadn't ever occurred to her—or if something else was worrying them, or if it was just the way her day had been set up.

By the time the last person left, she asked, "Could you close the door? I'll sleep now."

The woman smiled, nodded, and closed the door for her.

And, with that, Yvonne closed her own eyes and once again tried to sleep. Instead of sleep, all she saw was Dennis's face as she had walked away from him five years ago. She always refused to revisit that memory so it never bothered her, not until she had to come back here. She had been okay to bury what she could and did bury all this time that she had been gone because she didn't see him and didn't have to face him or to face her life *without him.*

Her life had been too busy. Her life had been good. She had been busy doing things. She was living life the way she was meant to live it. Until she wasn't. And now, for the first time, she realized what life was all about when you were alone. And the trouble was, she had nobody to blame but herself.

All this sounded as if she were some poor-me woman instead of the woman who had made very strong, clear decisions to lead her life this way. And yet here she was. A mess, once again. And, with that, she rolled over, punched her pillow a couple times to make it a little bit easier to sleep, closed her eyes, and finally slipped under.

DENNIS KEPT AN eye on Yvonne day in and day out. He got a little bit closer to her and then sensed the same walls as before. After lunch one day, he determined to sort out what was going on and sighed as he sat down beside her.

She looked up at him. "Tough day?" she ventured.

He smiled. "Well, tough something or another." He took a big breath and plunged in. "I want us to be friends."

She nodded immediately. "I would like us to be friends too."

"Yet it feels as if, every time I sit down by you, you're bracing yourself for something I might say."

She stared at him, her jaw dropping.

He studied her for a moment. "I call them as I see them."

"Sure, but I have to admit I had forgotten just how abrupt you can be."

"I don't think it's abrupt," he clarified. "You've been here three weeks already, if not four, and it still feels as if we're not comfortable around each other."

It was obvious she didn't know what to say about it.

He stared off into the distance, his mood dark, and yet he knew it was his fault, not hers. "I don't know what I can do to make the transition to friendship easier. I've been trying to stay out of your way. I know this is a tough time for you, and I'm not here to stress you out even more," he declared in a determined tone.

She frowned at him. And then her lips twitched.

He nodded. "But I am, aren't I?" he asked, with a heavy sigh. When she burst out laughing, he grinned at her. "See? I always loved that about you, that great sense of humor. Even when I messed up, you were always there with quick forgiveness."

"You never messed up," she replied, with a shake of her head. "I did. But you? You were always perfect."

He stared at her and then, feeling some of the stress inside easing slightly, he added, "None of us are perfect. How about we go with that," he suggested.

"I broke your heart," she said abruptly.

He winced and nodded. "Yep, you sure did. But obviously it wasn't the right time or it wasn't the right thing for us to be together," he said. "I've made peace with it over the time. You don't have to be afraid that I'll jump the gun or crowd you or push you into anything that you don't want to do. That's not who I am."

She nodded. "I know, and you're right. I was tensing every time you came around because there's an awful lot you could say to me, and I wouldn't blame you in the least. It still doesn't mean that I want to hear it."

He studied her for a long moment, knowing where she was going with this and realizing that he really needed to just let her off the hook. "I was hurt, yes," he agreed, "but I'm a big boy, and I understood at the time that I needed to let you go. So I did, but I still care about you, and I still want to see you do the best you can here. Yet the circumstances are very different for you now, and I've changed. You've changed."

"Yeah, and some of that change has not been for the good."

"I don't know about that," he replied. "I think the change as needed is definitely for the good. It's just sometimes hard because the change comes from experience. When you were here before, you were broken, emotionally, mentally, physically, struggling with the future of your life as it was then, the loss of a career that you adored, the loss of the life that you adored, and you were grieving. I couldn't help you grieve any faster. That was a process you needed to go through on your own. And I couldn't do anything but be there for you. I wanted to be there the whole time for you, but that obviously"—he gave a dismissive wave of his hand—"wasn't happening. And I promise I won't keep bringing that up."

Her lips twitched again, and he grinned.

"You're different now." He hesitated and then continued. "You're wiser. You're not as broken, but today it's as if you've hit a wall, a major wall that you never expected. There's almost a defeated attitude to you that wasn't there before. You were always gung-ho about beating this and being strong and invincible and finding that life that you so wanted and being determined to make a life for yourself. Yet this time I'm not seeing that same will, that same determination," he murmured. "So I know that the years in between have been hard and that you've learned some very tough lessons. Maybe I'm wrong about that. Maybe you've just been kicked down by life, and the lessons haven't been learned, but they're still there staring you in the face, and you just don't want to deal with them."

"Oh Lord," she muttered, staring at him. "I forgot how perceptive you are."

He shook his head. "I spend a lot of time watching humanity. I spend a lot of time watching people struggle, knowing that, if they would just reach out a hand, we could make it a little easier for them. But it's so limiting for us because, if we help too early, it's not something that you've achieved yourself. Yet, if we help too late, often we are literally too late, and you've lost that sense of purpose and that glow of accomplishment. So we struggle to try and get it back again and to re-energize you into wanting to care."

She smiled. "Let's unpack all that a little bit." She lifted her fingers and ticked them off. "One, yes, last time I was bound and determined to make the most of it. I refused to be one of those unable to accept what life had shot at me. I would accept it, and I would do my darndest to make a good life for myself. And, two, yes," she added, ticking off another finger, "I got kicked down in the world." She spoke with a sad tone to her voice. "I didn't really expect that. I didn't really see it coming, but, before I realized it, I was exhausted and worn out and scrambling to stay ahead. I don't think any of it had to do with my energy or my injury. I think a lot of it just had to do with the IT field I chose, the people I worked with, all of that. And it wasn't easy. A lot of it was just definitely not easy to live with," she murmured. "And before I realized it, I was already looking at how to get out of this profession. But instead of getting out, I had an accident that put me right back where I left."

"Except different," he reminded her.

"Except different," she agreed, with a nod. "I'm not sure the differences are any easier though," she murmured. "And that makes it very hard too."

"Of course it does, and I'm so sorry."

She nodded. "I thank you for that. I'm in a new adjustment period, and I promise you that, this time, if you reach out a helping hand, I will accept it very gratefully," she shared. "It is not an easy thing to admit, but I made a lot of mistakes last time because I thought I needed to do it all myself. I thought that I had to do it myself or else I wouldn't survive out there because I would always be dependent on everybody here. And honestly, that's not true."

She lifted her fingers to tick off the next point, then shook her head. "I don't even know what number we're on," she said, "but the bottom line is, I have changed, and maybe I have been beaten down by the reality of what life is like out there. It also probably would have been a huge shock for me if I had gone from working in the navy to real life even without the injury anyway," she suggested.

"But going solo as I did just accented the magnitude of the differences between what I had before and what I have now. … And then I had the next accident. And now, yeah, a part of me says, *I can't do this again*," she murmured. "A part of me says I'm not strong enough. A part of me says I don't want to do this all over again. And I, … I have to get over that. I have to get past that, and I don't know how." She sighed as she looked at him. "And do you realize I haven't told anybody any of this yet?" she asked.

"Oh, I think most of them already know," he pointed out, with a gentle smile. "Because, once again, what you have failed to realize is that you are not alone here. You have people to talk to, who can help you deal with small things, like picking up a pen from the floor, plus the larger things, like having help with personal hygiene when you're back in a wheelchair. The people here are pros at it. Many people here live with it on a daily basis. It's not easy, but it is definitely necessary for you to get your confidence back."

"It's not even my confidence," she said, staring at him. "I'm almost at a loss to know what to call it." And then she nodded. "*Chutzpah*. I've lost my chutzpah for life."

Chapter 6

I T WAS DAYS later until Yvonne saw Dennis again. She'd not been feeling well and had stayed in bed, with everybody else running around trying to help her out. So she hadn't called Dennis. And yet she should have. She knew he would be more than happy to bring her a coffee, but again she was struggling with that whole self-sufficient idea of how she should do it on her own.

The trouble was, as she had already found out, she wasn't capable of doing a lot of this on her own. She shifted in bed, already feeling the pain crouching inside her system. It was so much more painful this time. Then she had to stop at that thought. Was it the truth? She wasn't sure that it was. Was it really that much more painful, or was she just not as capable of handling the daily pain this time around?

She was tired. Was that it? She was tired of the fight, and she was tired of life. And that sounded as if she was pathetic, and she didn't want that at all. She didn't want to be somebody looking for handouts or looking for an easy answer because she wasn't that kind of person. But this time around she'd really lost her chutzpah, her love of life, her ability to get out of bed and to say, *Yes, I got this*.

Instead she got out of bed, cursing that she was awake again. And she had a whole new day ahead of her, even if she didn't want to face it. She had mentioned these revelations to her therapist, the day after speaking with Dennis about them, and the therapist had been absolutely thrilled that Yvonne had finally vocalized them. Yvonne admitted that she had figured it out while talking to Dennis.

Dr. Sandy Neeshorn had laughed. "You talk to whomever you need to talk to," she suggested, "because, in this place, everybody has insights, like you would not believe. So, when you find any insights, let's come back here, and we can hash them all out again. Don't feel guilty for figuring these things out with somebody else. Just ensure that you keep me in the loop, so that I know where your thoughts are and where you're going with them."

"I'm not going anywhere yet," she'd reassured her. "It was just an understanding that life as I had thought it would be just wasn't. And that sense of depression about it all."

And Dr. Sandy nodded. "And that makes a lot of sense too. Nobody wants to be in this position. Nobody wants to go through what you've already gone through once, much less a second time. That's just not in the cards for most of us, but the fact is, you did recover. You did go on to do things that you really wanted to do. So, if you change your mind now about what you want to do careerwise, that's okay too."

"Is it though?" she asked. "My job is very stressful, isolated, and I'm not really sure I'm cut out for it."

"Good. You see something that needs to be changed. So what would you be cut out for doing?"

"I don't know. I was so focused on the big picture, I wasn't thinking about my heart and my soul and what I might need to do just for my own sake, instead of that whole *I'll be a success in spite of myself* thing."

And now, the next morning, still in bed, Yvonne groaned, as her physical body argued with her pretty well about moving. Didn't matter. Moving or not, Yvonne was in pain. She rubbed her chest, wishing that everything didn't hurt. Still, she sat up slowly, wondering if she could make it to the shower. She was already late for Shane's appointment and knew that he would be there awaiting her. She'd missed breakfast too. When a knock came almost immediately on her door, she groaned. "Yeah, come in."

Shane poked his head around her door and frowned. "Bad night?"

"You could say that."

He nodded, stepped forward, and asked, "Where's the pain?"

She massaged her rib area and around her back. He frowned at that, obviously not happy. She nodded. "I know. I know, but I'm not sure what to do about it."

He sighed. "Take it easy today, and we'll see how you do tomorrow."

"If you're okay with that, I would appreciate it," she muttered. "I keep thinking each day how I should be doing better, but instead I feel as if I'm doing worse this time around."

"It's not a competition," he reminded her. "Not at all. It's a matter of doing what you need to do, and right now you need to spend the day in bed."

She nodded. "I just don't want to be waited on."

"Can you make your way down to the dining room and get some food and come back?"

She considered it and nodded. "I could probably do that, maybe."

And he shook his head. "No, I'll go get your food right now. And a coffee?"

She hesitated.

"Stop that right now. You're not looking well at all," he stated bluntly. "Get yourself back under the covers, ease up that chest, liver, whatever is causing you the most pain right now, and work on calming down your stress. I can see your heart rate and blood pressure already rising because of this pain, so I will get you breakfast and coffee." And, with that, and not giving her a chance to argue, he headed out of her room to the dining area.

She followed his instructions but struggled to even get comfortable again in bed.

When he returned with a plate of eggs and bacon and sausages and pancakes, she stared at it. "So were you thinking to feed both of us or what?"

He chuckled. "When you're hungry, you're hungry. And, if you are, then eat. If you're not, then don't."

She groaned. "I hate to waste food."

"And that's hardly the issue right now." He studied her face.

"Hey, I followed orders," she declared, at least sitting in bed now.

"Yeah? But you don't look anywhere near better."

"Yeah, well, I'm working on it." She moved the small table closer to her. "Thanks."

"I'll come back in a bit." And, with that, he took off.

She ate about half of the food and then pushed away the table, as the pain started to build. She got up and walked around, looked out the window, trying to ease up whatever was bothering her spine. Maybe not even her spine but something wasn't quite right.

When someone knocked on her door, she turned suddenly. The door opened, and she stood there, gasping in pain, as Dennis took one look and raced over and held her upright. "God," she cried out, "the pain, the pain." She took one step toward the bed. Then she whispered, "Oh God," and collapsed.

DENNIS HAD THE Hathaway doctors at Yvonne's side within minutes and stepped out of the way, watching as everybody worked on her. He wasn't exactly sure what was going on, but Shane stepped into the room and called him outside.

"Come on out here, big guy. You're in the way."

When Dennis stepped into the hallway, he asked Shane, "What happened?"

"I don't know for sure. She's stable. She's going back to the nearest hospital, which will be a civilian hospital this time. Hopefully they will find out more while she's there."

Dennis frowned, his heart sinking. "She'll hate that."

"She might hate it, but something major is going on, and I think it's the shrapnel."

"Ah, shoot," he murmured.

"I know. I know. But this is one of those things that she should probably deal with first."

"You know that she'll hate going through another surgery, seeing it as just ten more steps backward."

"Yep, that part she'll hate all right," Shane agreed. "However, I think she really wants the shrapnel dealt with. While we all don't like hearing what's currently happening, we can't take a chance of not getting her treated right away."

"I know," he whispered.

The ambulance was already here by the time Dennis turned around, as he watched her get loaded onto a gurney. "That was fast," he muttered.

"We do keep them on call for emergencies when needed," Shane explained. "Dani is already wondering about having one here on standby, at the ready. We shouldn't have to. It's not for accidents. It's for problems like this, where a patient needs surgery, because we're not set up for that. Still, every once in a while, we must take somebody to the hospital, and you always wonder how you can make that transit time go that much faster."

Dennis followed the EMTs to the front reception area, as they guided Yvonne to the ambulance. Shane was at his side, as they stood and watched her get loaded inside and then drove off. Dennis wrapped his arms around his chest. "Will you keep me informed?"

"I will. Go keep yourself busy. Do something to take your mind off this."

Dennis rolled his eyes. "I'll go to the kitchen. They're trying to teach me to cook some of the dishes."

"If you want to learn how to make cinnamon buns, that would be good." Shane waggled his eyebrows. "*Huh? Huh?*"

Dennis laughed. "In other words, I should be learning about sweets. Is that it?"

"None of us will ever say no to that, and you know that there's never enough either. Those cinnamon buns are gone almost instantly, and even our esteemed leader doesn't get one every time we have them."

At that somebody behind them cried out, "Were there cinnamon buns today, and I didn't get any?"

They turned, smirking, as Dani stared at them.

Shane nudged Dennis. "See? That's what I mean. If the boss lady can't even get a cinnamon bun …"

Dennis shook his head at Shane's antics. "No cinnamon buns today, Dani. Shane's just suggesting I go keep occupied by learning to make some."

Dani nodded. "I will second that motion." She rubbed her hands together. "And, if we know that you're making them today"—she looked down at her watch—"should I come see you in about an hour and a half?" she asked. "I could get one this time."

Shane grinned. "There, Dennis. You're kinda hooked into it now."

"I'll see what Ilse is up to," Dennis replied, as he took off. "You guys are *not* suffering for a lack of cinnamon buns."

"No, but we're not exactly overwhelmed with them either," Dani called out.

Dennis raced to the kitchen. He still heard the two of them talking and laughing behind him. And he knew what they were trying to do, but still it was a good thing on their part, distracting him. According to them, they were shorted on cinnamon buns. When he mentioned that to Ilse, she snorted at him.

"They'll do anything to get us to make another batch."

"And I agree with them," Dennis said. "I desperately need something to do."

"Outside of handling everything out there?"

"Yes, I won't be going to bed at all tonight, not until I have answers."

"I'm sorry about Yvonne's setback, buddy. So, you want to learn how to make cinnamon buns?"

He grinned. "How hard are they?"

"Not at all. Our pastry chef isn't here right now, but I certainly have a good old-fashioned recipe we can use. I have Danish ones," she added, thinking about it. "I've been wanting to make those."

"We'll make a double batch," he suggested. "I'll make one as you make one."

"Perfect. Can't say I've ever taught that way."

"I learn better by doing it myself," Dennis said. "And Lord knows I need to be doing something right now."

"Have faith that it'll work out for Yvonne."

And, with that, Ilse turned Dennis's attention to grabbing a big mixing bowl. With the kitchen help laughing and teasing the two of them, Ilse showed Dennis how to make Danish cinnamon buns.

Chapter 7

WHEN YVONNE WOKE, she rolled her head to the side, noting she was in a hospital bed with railings up on both sides. Frowning, she tried to figure out where she was. White walls, white sheets, no window. Well, there was a window, but it was so small and so high up the wall as to not really count. And many other hospital beds were all in this same room. She closed her eyes, as all the details drifted through her sleepy drug-induced brain, and she realized she was back in a hospital, a civilian hospital. She groaned as the pain started to infiltrate her consciousness.

Almost immediately a nurse stepped forward and asked, "How're you doing?" She slipped on a blood pressure cuff and started running Yvonne through a battery of tests.

"I don't feel so hot," she murmured.

"You had an unexpected surgery," she stated.

Yvonne opened her eyes and frowned. "Pardon?"

"I'll let the doctor tell you about it. He'll be here in a few minutes. Once I realized you were awake, I called him," she explained. "So just hold tight, and we'll explain it to you. In the meantime, I'll get you some water and something for the pain." And she quickly disappeared.

Yvonne sighed, trying to understand what all had just happened.

A doctor walked to her, took one look, and smiled.

"There you are," he greeted her. "Darn good thing you were where you were when you collapsed," he began. "Hathaway House had you to us in no time."

"I was at Hathaway," she noted, then frowned. "Wasn't I?"

"Yes, you were, indeed. Glad you remember that much."

"I don't remember much else though," she replied cautiously, "and I certainly don't remember arriving at the hospital."

"What do you remember?" he asked.

"Just pain. Dennis trying to get me to the bed so I could lie down," she muttered, fighting back the memories. "And me collapsing."

"That's pretty well what happened," he confirmed. "They had you moved to the hospital pretty fast, so the end result was you no longer have shrapnel moving around in your body."

She stared at him in shock.

"Yes, we took it out. The one at the liver had already cut in and was working some nasty pace deeper into that organ, causing a lot of internal bleeding, not to mention the pain you must have had," he shared. "We managed to extract it, and, while we were in there, we took out the other one close to your spine. I have done that multiple times because I deal with Hathaway patients a lot. Although it's not the kind of experience I expected to get, they have given me more cases than I had ever thought to have in my lifetime," he murmured. "But, between them and others in the past, you got the benefit of that expertise. So," he added, studying her, "what I really want to know is …" He poked her toes on each foot ever-so-gently.

She shifted her legs to get away from him.

He smiled. "And that is magic to my eyes."

"What is?"

"When you moved your feet."

"Yes, of course I did." Then she stared at him, her eyes wide. "Oh my gosh, I'm not paralyzed."

"Nope, you're sure not," he declared. "However, that bleeding in your liver is something that we can't fool around with, so you're staying here for a couple days. When I see that everything is solid and ready to go, you can return to Hathaway House."

His words crashed through her brain. "I can go back?" she repeated, tears in her eyes.

He nodded. "But first we have to ensure there's no ongoing damage to the liver."

"Right," she muttered. "I don't want that. Does that mean the crushing pain I felt all the time is gone?"

"Sure should be gone, at least from the shrapnel," he clarified. "I can't guarantee your other injuries won't cause some other pain," he added.

"No, of course not." She gave him a wave of her hand. "And I don't expect that. But I'm so grateful to have that shrapnel out."

"I'm sure you are," he agreed. "With modern medicine, we can finally make some headway on some of these injuries that not everybody is as comfortable doing the surgery on. In my case, well, I've done them a time or two, so the more often I get to work with some of these injuries, the better off the patients are."

"Absolutely," she murmured.

"Besides, I'm also a really good surgeon." And, with that, he gave her a cheerful grin and disappeared.

The nurse returned almost immediately, clucking

around Yvonne as if a mother hen. "He's really happy with your progress. And apparently you're not even experiencing any temporary paralysis."

"None," Yvonne said, with a smile. "I don't know if I should laugh or cry." The tears were already in her eyes.

"I suspect for a while you'll do both," the nurse suggested. "It must be a huge relief to get that out of there."

"It is," Yvonne agreed. "I can't believe that it all happened, and I, … I wasn't even aware of it."

"When these emergencies happen, it is what it is," she noted. "In this case, it's all good. And, by the way, people from Hathaway House have called several times to see how you're doing."

"I'm sure they have," she noted.

"I believe Dani will be here later today to check up on you."

Yvonne sniffled at that. "Dani's one heck of a woman," she murmured.

"She is, indeed," the nurse stated, with a smile. "We do see her on an irregular occasion, dealing with various patients. She's a mother hen, trying to get everybody back to her place again."

At that, Yvonne laughed and then stopped laughing, groaning with pain instead.

"Right? Don't forget. You just had surgery. We had to cut you open to get in there," she explained, "so it'll be a little while yet before you get to laugh without feeling it."

"But I will laugh again, and that is huge."

At that, the nurse smiled and patted her hand. "I totally agree. Now let's get this medicine down you, and then sleep as much as you can," she urged her patient. "The best thing you can do for yourself right now is get as much rest as you can handle." Reminding Yvonne to push the Call button, as needed, the nurse took off.

"Good Lord," Yvonne whispered to herself, as she stared around the room she shared with other people in the nearby hospital beds. Yvonne smiled, her heart full and cheerful. On her bedside table was her phone. She hesitated, then picked it up, and looked to see if she had Dennis's number. Of course she did. It was there from years before, a number she had yet to get rid of.

She sent him a quick text. **I'm awake. Shrapnel, both pieces, are gone. Looks like I made it safely on the other side.** Then she collapsed onto the bed, waiting and hoping for an answer. When she finally got one, it brought tears to her eyes.

Love you. Take care. He added a big heart emoji too.

That was Dennis. He never held back. She had always been the one who held back, not him. He'd been open and honest, and she'd been dedicated to her future. How could she have walked away from something so precious? She didn't know. And even now, lying here in the hospital, she had to wonder if there was any chance of going backward and getting the real thing out of this relationship that she desperately wanted, which was with Dennis. Somewhere along the line she'd taken a wrong turn in life, and right now all she could think about was how this might be the opportunity to make it all better.

Now that she was back where she started some five years earlier, could she revisit that long-ago decision and make a right turn this time?

THE NEXT DAY Dennis reached for his phone, as he sat on the deck all alone in the early morning hour. Some days were just too nice to spend inside. Everybody was busy in the kitchen before breakfast started. This was his first few moments to himself. He'd already called the hospital, unbeknownst to Yvonne, but he just had to check. When his phone rang, he looked down to see her number show up. "Yvonne? Are you all right?" he asked hesitantly.

"I'm better than all right," she replied. "Both pieces of shrapnel are out."

He closed his eyes in relief. "That is, indeed, good news. Any further damage?"

"The liver's lacerated," she murmured. "So I'm staying here, until they're sure that everything there is fine. Other than that, it looks as if I'm good to go."

"And that is huge news," he murmured.

"It is, indeed," she declared, a smile in her tone again. "I didn't realize just how much having that in there was bothering me."

"I can't imagine that it would have been very pleasant."

"Right, and the surgeon says that was most likely the cause of the sharp pain I was always experiencing. Of course he can't guarantee that something else isn't going on, but he couldn't find anything else wrong."

"And that is great news," Dennis said, a bright smile on his face. "So you won't be back today?"

"Not today, not tomorrow. I think they'll keep me in over the weekend, and then potentially I'll be back Monday, Tuesday—except I'm not sure if I can start rehab right away."

"Well, this isn't the first time we've sent a patient to the hospital for one reason or another," Dennis pointed out, "so

I'm sure Dani will figure it out."

"Is it okay if I'm staying there for possibly a week or two before I can do much rehab with Shane?"

"I'm sure you'll be doing something," he replied. "However, the scope of what you do will be changing."

There was silence on the other end, as she pondered that.

He smiled, reaching up to stop the tears that he hadn't even realized were forming in his eyes. "I'm sure it'll be fine. If you want, I can talk to Dani about it."

"Would you mind?"

"No, of course not. I'll go check and see if she's there now, and you can hold on the line."

"I don't want to disturb you. I'm sure you're getting ready for breakfast."

"I was just sitting out on the deck, having my few minutes."

"I remember how you used to do that," she murmured.

"Yep," he said, with a chuckle. "I still do it. It's that few magical moments before the day starts." He was already walking down the hallway toward Dani's office. Hearing her voice, he followed the sound until he got to the front reception area, where she stood, talking to Amanda.

At the sight of him, Dani looked up, raised an eyebrow. "And?"

"And," he said, waving his phone around, "Yvonne's here right now on the phone. She's doing much better. Both pieces of shrapnel are out. The hospital will keep her over the weekend. She's concerned that she can't come back here because she won't start doing her normal rehab until her surgeon clears it."

Dani just rolled her eyes and then chuckled and held out

her hand.

Dennis told Yvonne, "Hang on a minute. Dani wants to speak with you." He handed the phone over and waited, listening to half the conversation, as Dani reassured Yvonne that her bed was here and ready and that rehab would happen when she was physically cleared, and that was it. That went for everybody on the floor, no matter what the problem was that set them back. And, when they finally had reassured Yvonne, Dani returned Dennis's phone to him.

Dani glanced at the wall clock behind him and teased Amanda, "Now I'll go steal a cinnamon bun or two because Dennis isn't there to stop us." And, with that, she made a quick cartoony dash around Dennis and raced down the hallway.

Laughing, Dennis added to Yvonne, "As much as I hate to end this phone call, I do need to get ready to serve breakfast."

"Absolutely," Yvonne agreed, an obvious relief in her tone. "I'm really looking forward to coming back." And, with that, she disconnected.

He wasn't even sure what to think about that, but anything that made her want to come back would make him happy.

As he headed into the kitchen with a big smile on his face, Ilse took one look and declared, "That's an indicator of good news if I ever saw one."

He flashed a grin at her. "Yvonne's doing fine. Both pieces of shrapnel are gone now, and she'll be in the hospital over the weekend and then back home."

"When you say *home*, you mean here?" she asked, one eyebrow raised.

"Yes," he replied, trying not to flush at what was an obvious response on his part because this was *his* home. He lived and worked here, in many ways beyond what most people would consider the norm. But Yvonne coming *home* was an indicator of a much bigger problem. And it was obvious that Ilse knew it too.

She eyed him warily.

He shrugged. "Hey, it is what it is. I almost married the woman."

She nodded. "And I suspect there'll be happy nuptials in your future soon."

"I don't know about that," he noted, with a warning. "She hasn't given any indication that we can be anything but friends, and I'm the one who had to ask if we could go back to being that." When Ilse stared at him, he shrugged. "It seemed as if every time I got close to her, she was tensing."

"Ah, yep, have to love that fear factor."

"Right?" he replied. "And I was just as guilty. I didn't want to talk to her and start something, or set her off, or upset her in any way. So I was just relegated to watching from a distance."

"True." She shook her head. "Well, at least we got cinnamon buns out of you." He laughed. "Now, are you ready to get your regular day started?"

"I'm always ready," Dennis declared, as he took out several large trays and placed them in the big serving counter outside.

A lineup was already forming. As soon as he showed up with food, a cheer rang out. He rolled his eyes. "Hey, I'm all of two minutes late, guys."

"Hey, two minutes for you, that's like waiting a lifetime," joked one of the guys in front of the line. "You know how much we enjoy our food here."

"I do, indeed," Dennis confirmed. "Let me grab the rest of it."

As he turned around, Ilse and the rest of the kitchen staff were bringing out the remaining dishes. And, with the buffet counter finally loaded up, Dennis started serving. Once it got busy, it stayed busy for hours. When he turned around, it was 10:30 a.m. already. He shook his head as he looked at Ilse. "The days sometimes just go by in a flash."

"I think the days always just go by," she stated, blowing loose strands of hair off her face. "Now, you'll be okay for the rest of the day?" she asked.

"I'll be okay for the rest of the week," he declared, chuckling. "Nothing like a spot of good news to keep one buoyant." And, with that, he turned to deal with the rest of his day.

Chapter 8

FEELING BETTER, AT least emotionally, Yvonne spent the next three days healing, resting, doing some more healing, and sleeping as much as she could. Her back was still sore, but she no longer had that sharp pain, which didn't happen every time she moved but happened just enough times to wonder, *Would it be okay or not to move?* And now, with both pieces of shrapnel gone, she felt much more reassured about everything.

As it was, when Monday dawned bright and early, and the doctor cleared her to return to Hathaway, she could hardly wait to phone Dani to arrange for a ride. After the call, Yvonne felt even better. They would come and get her right away. Of course the hospital needed the bed too.

As she said goodbye to the hospital staff, Yvonne spoke to the kind nurse who'd been looking after her for the last two days. "Nothing personal," Yvonne told her, "but I really hope I don't have to come back."

The nurse laughed. "Hey, we don't take it personally. And, in this place, considering the pain that brought you in," she noted, "we do understand. We want you to move on and to have a long healthy life without any more hospital visits."

And, with that, Yvonne turned to see Dani standing in the doorway. Her jaw dropped. "You?"

"What's the matter?" Dani joked. "Do you think I don't

do transfers? The doctor told me how you didn't need an ambulance, so I'm here to take you back."

Yvonne was wheeled out in a wheelchair by the weekend nurse to a large SUV, then helped into the front passenger seat. Dani proceeded to drive them from the hospital parking lot to head home.

"Wow," Yvonne muttered, "I didn't expect to put you out."

"You didn't put me out," Dani clarified, glancing at her. "It's just one of the many hats I wear."

Yvonne nodded. "I just thought it would be somebody else."

"Well, believe me that Dennis would've come, if I could've spared him, but that wouldn't work with lunch happening."

She laughed at that. "No, Dennis is pretty vital."

"It's funny," Dani began in a contemplative tone as they drove. "The actual job he does, I could probably get any number of people to handle without very many technical skills or much experience. However, the actual role he plays is a very different story."

Yvonne frowned, considering that. "I never thought of it that way."

"Dennis is part of the heart of the Hathaway House community," Dani declared. "Or maybe I should say, he's the soul. Everything he does, he does with love. He doesn't cook the food, although I understand from Ilse he's been taking all kinds of cooking lessons lately. Normally he plates it and handles all the patients as if they are the one and only one in rehab at our place. Everybody responds to his particular version of our community." And, with that, Dani lapsed into silence, as she navigated through traffic.

To Yvonne, the Hathaway House *community* was something odd for her to contemplate, but Dani was right. Dennis was an integral part of the place, something that Yvonne hadn't necessarily seen before. He'd been her friend—her special friend in many ways, her potential partner. So, when she'd turned down his offer of marriage, she hadn't really considered that her rejection would reverberate onto everybody else.

No doubt all of those at Hathaway House knew in one way or another that he had asked her to marry him. No reason for them to have not known because she and Dennis had been seen together constantly. But five years ago, Yvonne just hadn't been ready. And now she wondered if she would ever get another chance. There was just something so very special about him. And she didn't even know where she stood with him or even where he stood with her.

Sure, he had said *Love you* in a recent text, but Yvonne had had friends and family do that too. She wanted that special *in love with you* kind of love. In her own mind they were still a mess, mostly because of her guilt for not taking him up on his offer five years ago. And here she was, heading back into his healing embrace in so many ways, and yet not in the way she wanted. In her heart, she didn't feel as if she deserved a second chance. She looked over at Dani. "Do you think everybody deserves a second chance?"

Dani nodded. "And a third and fourth and fifth and sixth," she replied instantly.

That burbled a laugh out of Yvonne. "Really?"

"Yep. Some people are slower learners. Some people don't understand the message. Sometimes it takes them a little longer to get it. Sometimes they have to learn the hard way. Sometimes they make a mistake, and they didn't learn all of what they needed to. Thus, they have to make another mistake to get the rest of it," Dani explained. "Who are we to judge?"

"I guess I hadn't considered that quite in the same light."

"And you're thinking about Dennis, aren't you?"

She flushed as she saw Dani's knowing gaze. "I guess everybody knows, don't they?"

"Not everybody, but a lot of the old-timers? Sure. We knew how it was between the two of you before."

"And yet I turned him down," she muttered softly.

Dani nodded slowly. "I know, and it was the right thing for you to do."

Shocked, she stared at her. "What? How can you say that?" she cried out.

Dani's lips twitched. "Obviously you're having second thoughts now," she pointed out, "but in reality you weren't ready five years ago. The fact that you turned him down meant you weren't ready. For a lot of people, what Dennis offered was a massive gift, a huge boon to what so many women would want, but it wasn't what you wanted at the time," Dani offered.

"Now, I'm not judging you. I'm not saying anything about that in any way, shape, or form. But, for you, back then, you needed to go out into the big wide world and still learn more about yourself. I think you have done that now. I don't know where you and Dennis are at in this present moment, and it doesn't matter because that's your problem. It's not ours. It took me a long and twisted road to get to where I am. And the fact that I'm making wedding plans and booking flowers for my own wedding, that's enough to even think that I've come this far." She sighed.

"Yet it feels as if I'm very overdue, and I should've just

walked into a minister's office and got it done years ago," she shared. "But Aaron wanted to finish school, and that was fine. In hindsight, I would much prefer to have been living with him as his wife all this time, instead of waiting until he was done."

"Oh, I can see that," Yvonne agreed. "I was quite surprised when I heard how long you've been together."

"Right?" Dani said, with a chuckle. "But you make these decisions, and then afterward you look back, and you think, *What was so important?* And we decided what was really important was that we had time together whenever possible within this long-distance relationship. Obviously we had time together, and maybe—I won't say *probably*—but maybe it was easier this way. We certainly enjoyed every moment we had together, and being married won't change that. Yet, if anything happens between now and then, I'll be incredibly sad to not have been his wife in the meantime," she admitted.

"Also I knew my father wanted me to have a big wedding, and he wanted to walk me down the aisle. So mostly I think—partly because of Hathaway House—that I did hold off because so many people wanted to attend our wedding. And, if I had just gone into a minister's office and got it done, I don't think that would have had quite the same effect or had the same response from everybody here. They're all busy planning the entire thing, and that's both fun and also kind of scary." Dani laughed.

"I like the fun part. We are still struggling to get everything lined up. We'll get married at Hathaway House, obviously. Ilse and Dennis had been working on the menu in a frenzy, even though the event is not for a couple months yet. *Wow, okay, guys. Remember a budget is involved here.* But they seem to think that Hathaway House should absorb part of that budget. I already feel bad because my staff people are doing this on their own hours off." And then she let her voice trail off.

That was something Yvonne hadn't even considered. "Just so much is involved in this that you don't think about, from the outside looking in, isn't there?"

"And yet really the bottom line is you want to spend—*I*," Dani corrected, "I want to spend every moment that I can with Aaron. The fact that he's coming back and will be working with Stan is absolutely breathtaking for me. The fact that Stan desperately needs the help right now is also a good thing, and he's trying to ease back some of his workload so that he can spend more time with his new partner." Dani smiled.

"In the last few years so many couples came together here at Hathaway House," she stated, "that we feel truly blessed. As well as healing people, a harmony is here, an openness is here. Sure we have fights, we have disagreements, we have jealousy, we have, in some cases, sheer ignorance of how things operate or how people are progressing faster than others, and a constant reminder to always communicate better," she murmured. "However, we've also witnessed so much healing, so much emotional and physical healing, that I know in many ways we've created some little miracles here," she noted. "And, yeah, that's being very arrogant ..."

"No," Yvonne countered. "I wouldn't say *arrogance* at all. *Confidence* maybe, because really, you should be proud of everything you have done here."

"I am," Dani agreed. She pointed up ahead. "And here's our turnoff."

As Dani navigated onto the long driveway to the property ahead of them, Yvonne muttered, "It feels like coming home, doesn't it?"

Dani looked at her and chuckled. "You're not the first person to say that. In many cases it has become home. We have expanded a lot of our employee housing to be big enough for couples. I've got single housing units always turning over as some staff move to town with new partners or their partners are in town already so they move in with them. I have some of the partners who were patients here, who stayed because that was convenient, depending on the work their significant others were doing," she added, with a smile. "It's always been fascinating to me to see what arrangements people make in order to have something work for them."

Yvonne frowned. "I never even thought of that. I was so focused on taking on the world and showing them that my injuries wouldn't hold me back that I didn't even think about life past that challenge. I was thinking ... I would just be *it*. I was the next *it* girl," she shared, with a bitter laugh.

At that Dani gently clasped her hand with hers. "Don't be so bitter about it. You needed to learn something, something that was important to you. I hope you've learned it. I hope that whatever you went through these last few years was worth it. And just remember that it's a never-ending process. When you work toward something, and you get it, then you find something else, and you work toward that." She chuckled. "There is no such thing as one endpoint. There are only stepping stones on this pathway of life."

"And what is your next stepping stone?" Yvonne asked Dani in amusement.

"First, I'll get married," she said, with an eye roll. "That seems to be a pretty major stepping point. And then maybe"—she smiled—"maybe I'll be lucky enough to start a family."

"Oh my," Yvonne replied, as images of tumbling toddlers running around Hathaway entered her imagination. "Can you imagine what that would do to the place?"

"Oh, I can." Dani laughed. "But don't forget that I have my own house on the property. And my father has his own cabin up there as well. So it's not as if the children will be in Hathaway House all the time. That might be good for patients to visit with the children every once in a while, but it could also be extremely hard on some," she noted. "We have to remember that a lot of these men have temporarily separated from their families so that they could get through these rehab sessions without interruption. So I must be judicious in my thought process as to how that could work."

"And again," Yvonne admitted, "I never even thought of that."

"No, but it's, … it's part and parcel of healing, isn't it?" Dani asked. "Everything I do is integrated with Hathaway House. But then I have to think about all the people who are here. And what they can and cannot do." She looked over at Yvonne. "Do you want children?"

"Nobody told me that I couldn't have children, at least not that I know of," Yvonne muttered, with a headshake. "It was something that concerned me last time, and then I shut it down, thinking it would never happen because, hey, I would be that big career woman again." She gave Dani an eye roll. "And now I find that I want something very different out of my life."

"And what is that?"

"I want peace," she replied. "I want to get up in the morning and not feel that same aggressive need to go out and to prove myself.”

“Oh, I agree with that,” Dani stated. “That sounds like an absolutely wonderful goal.”

“And,” Yvonne added, as Dani pulled up to the ramp at the front entrance, “to be perfectly honest, I want Dennis.”

DENNIS KNEW YVONNE was on her way back. He’d heard from the grapevine within minutes of Dani being picked as the transport driver. He walked out to the lobby several times to see if they had arrived.

Finally Ilse said, “Go and get a coffee and sit down and relax.” He just glared at her. She put her hands on her hips, and all five foot four of her stood nose to chest and issued her order. “Move it.”

And he’d moved it … because Ilse was right. He was completely of no use to her while he was mooning around, struggling to see Yvonne again. And so, with coffee in his hand, he checked the empty lobby, then went downstairs for a quick visit with Stan.

Stan took one look and asked, “Is she on her way back?”

He nodded glumly. “Ilse kicked me out.”

Stan laughed, his face splitting into a big grin. Then he dropped something huge and furry in Dennis’s arms and said, “Good. Look after this one for me.”

Dennis frowned down at it. “What the devil?” It was a raccoon.

“Yep, we call him Trash Panda,” Stan replied. “And unfortunately this one got into his owner’s trash. We had to clean out his stomach and pulled out … sixty-two bottle caps. His owner collects them and, for some reason, Trash

Panda swallowed them."

Dennis stared at Stan in shock and looked at Trash Panda in his arms, who was just grinning at him. Then the animal reached up and whacked him on the chin. "He's quite a character, isn't he?"

"You'll find that, once you get to know them, every animal has individual and completely different personalities," Stan declared, with a smile. "And this guy—his name is really George, by the way, as in Curious George, the monkey—is already quite a character."

"But he doesn't look to be suffering now."

"No, now that the incision has closed, I'll probably send him home tomorrow," Stan shared, "but that's only if the owner can keep him out of the garbage."

Dennis chuckled, and the raccoon stretched up to sniff Dennis's nose and mouth.

Stan asked, "You got food on you?"

"No, but I work in the kitchen, so I was just pulling cookies out of the oven and putting them on cooling racks," he murmured. "Then filling up the outside bins."

Stan watched the raccoon in Dennis's arms. "You may be his newest best friend, as this guy can spot food a mile away."

"He hasn't made it up to my dining room, so I'll take that as a good sign."

"No, and he doesn't do well in his cage. He gets really depressed, so we do try to get him out as much as we can."

"And does he have free reign at his home?"

"Yes, he does, inside and out. So, as much as I would like to tell off the homeowner for his too-easily available bottle cap collection, I'm not sure that this furry guy isn't getting them somewhere else."

With that, Dennis shook his head and continued to cuddle and pet the raccoon that appeared to be completely content to sit in his arms for the entire visit. When Stan finally reached out his arms, the raccoon walked right into them.

"He seems to know you."

"Oh, he knows me all right." Stan chuckled. "This is about the third, maybe the fourth, time he's been in to have his stomach emptied."

"Ouch," Dennis muttered, staring at the raccoon in amusement.

"Yeah." And even then the raccoon reached his arms around Stan's neck in a big hug. "He gets a tummy ache, and I have to come clean him out every once in a while," Stan shared, with a sigh. "You would think that, by now, he had learned to eat things that could go right through him."

"Not likely." Dennis laughed. "Chances are, he'll be back again, just so he could see you."

"Wouldn't that be something," Stan said, as he held the raccoon close. "Imagine an animal eating something wrong, just so he can come in and see me." He shook his head at that. "In which case his owner needs to spend a lot more time giving George some love and attention."

"Maybe point that out to the owner," Dennis suggested, with a grin. "You never know. And now I'll head back up and see if Yvonne's here."

"Yeah, but you know that she'll be ordered straight to her room to rest, after her road trip from the hospital back here."

Dennis nodded. "I still want to at least see her, to know that she's all right."

Stan nodded, with a sly grin. "It's been a whole twenty

minutes that you've been down here," Stan called out.

"Hey, twenty minutes is twenty minutes," Dennis murmured as he walked out.

Almost as soon as he got to the top of the stairs and entered the main hallway, he saw Racer sitting on the ground beside a man with no legs, also sitting on the ground beside him. Dennis stopped and asked him, "Did you need a hand?"

The man looked up and gave him a big toothy grin. "Nope, Racer and I are just having, … well, a race," he explained.

Dennis watched in astonishment, as the big man used his arms to drag his lower torso along, as he competed alongside Racer down the hallway, the little Chihuahua's wheels on his back end spinning as fast as they could go.

The big guy looked back over at Dennis and whispered, "I have to let the little guy win sometimes."

Dennis laughed. "Sure you do." And then the big guy's name popped into his head. "You're Olsen, aren't you?"

"Yep, sure am," he confirmed. "My prosthetics are acting up today," he explained. "They sored up my legs, so I took them off, and I'm out here just enjoying life, the same as Racer is."

Dennis nodded. "An awful lot can be said for being comfortable in your own skin, in your own physical condition, no matter what it is."

Olsen nodded. "And I used to be as big as you, but, even chopped in half, I'm still a big-enough force to be a contender to best Racer."

At that Racer came racing back, barking at him.

"And what's that for?" Dennis asked curiously.

"He's upset I didn't race him down the hallway. So,

Dennis, back to the kitchen with you. I'm working up a heck of an appetite, so we need to ensure there's food for us."

"Ha." Dennis chuckled. "Don't worry. I'll race you both down to the dining room." And with that, full-out breaking all the rules, he raced down the hallway, as Olsen fisted it all the way down, while Racer ran on his wheels. As Dennis reached the large dining room, a group of people stood outside the double doors.

They stopped, took one look, and started to laugh.

Dennis grinned. "Hey, they encouraged me to get back to the kitchen, so you guys could have lunch," he explained. "What could I do? Turn them down?"

"We agree with that, but that's not what we are laughing at," one of the women replied, a big grin on her face. "I'm laughing because Racer beat you."

And, sure enough, Racer still ran circles around Dennis's feet. "Hey, he's got wheels," Dennis protested.

"Yeah? And what about Olsen?"

Olsen sat there at the doorway too.

"All right, that's enough outta you guys," Dennis complained, then chuckled. "I'm heading into the kitchen now." And, with that, he returned to work.

Chapter 9

YVONNE OPENED HER eyes the next morning with a jolt, saw that she was again at Hathaway House, and sagged back into her bed with a big sigh. "Thank God," she whispered.

It was amazing just how much panic had set in when she had initially woken up in the civilian hospital, not only wondering what was going on but also worrying that she may not make it back to Hathaway House again. Somewhere along the line, coming back here had meant coming home to her, and it meant some kind of a return from a path that she'd taken a wrong turn on.

It made no sense, and she would probably be years, if not decades, working her way through it, but it just felt *right* to be here now. And knowing that she would get the care that she needed was also a huge plus. When a knock came on her door, she called out, "Come in."

Dennis stuck his head around the corner and smiled. "Ah, you're awake."

She smiled at him gently. "Of course you would be the first one here this morning," she teased.

He gave her a sheepish smile and held up a cup of coffee.

"Oh my." She reached out with both hands. "Gimme, gimme, gimme."

He laughed and came forward. "I wasn't sure if you

would even be awake yet," he admitted.

"And I probably shouldn't be," she noted, with a smile, "but I have to admit that the first thought I had when I woke up was, *Thank heavens I'm here.*"

He nodded in understanding. "That's the thing about this place. It really does grow on you."

"It grows on you too much in some ways," she admitted. "I'm wondering if I wasn't feeling just too dependent on that part before."

He frowned at her, his jaw half open, and then he slowly nodded. "That's … that's possible," he agreed, "and we don't really understand where our brain goes with some of this stuff until afterward."

"Back to that wise hindsight thing," she noted, with a smile.

"Absolutely, and it's not always that it's better or worse," he pointed out. "It's just different."

She had to agree. She held the cup of coffee close to her chest and sighed happily. "It is good to be back, though," she murmured. "Just something about knowing that I'll be safe here."

"And that's also an interesting phrase to use," he stated, studying her carefully. "Did the outside world feel *not safe?*"

She frowned at that. "I don't know where that *safe* issue is even coming from, from before," she clarified. "But I think going from being part of the navy, part of that whole big military machine, where you were answerable to everything that you did, gave me a whole plan already laid out for years. I had people to look after me. A system was in place. You didn't have to worry about falling through the cracks." She frowned. "And then, when I got out into the world all on my own, *all* on my own," she repeated with emphasis, "because of course I eschewed anybody's help, I found it scary, unnerving, and at times downright horrifying to realize just how different life was without that fallback position," she murmured.

"I can understand that too," Dennis agreed. "However, you're here now, and you're safe, and you're on the other side of surgery. So whatever time frame you need to get back on your feet should be all good."

"In this case, it is," she declared, with a smile. "I don't know where the insurance is at, and I can't say I'm too bothered at the moment, but hopefully everything will go through, and that won't even be part of my issue."

"I would hope not, especially with Dani overseeing every detail of that just so you don't have to," Dennis explained. "At the moment, the bottom line is you need to *not* worry about any of that, but just focus on getting on your feet, ready to tackle whatever comes next."

"And then we get back to my other problem—me not ready to tackle anything this time," she shared.

"Oh, I'm not so sure about that," he countered. "From what I heard, the surgery was a huge success. I would like to think that gives you more mobility, less pain—once you've fully recovered from the surgery itself—not to mention less meds, less painkillers. Who knows? Your touchy stomach may even clear up. Just think of how all that would improve your days, would give you more energy to spend on rehab, more incentive to rehab." Dennis gave her a huge smile.

Yvonne nodded. "Plus, no paralysis from the surgery. That alone relieves me of so much stress and worry. So, not only are my physical symptoms already better, but my mental and emotional responses have shifted, just like you said, so I can more fully focus on rehab." Yvonne smiled right back at him. She loved that Dennis always freely gave those big gentle teddy bear smiles.

"Good. Don't pressure yourself. Don't worry about things. Do what you can in rehab to find out where you're at in each moment," he suggested, "and the rest will fall into place." And, with that, he pointed to her door. "I have to go back to the kitchen. I'll come by in a bit and see what you want for breakfast."

"Or you can just bring me something," she suggested, "and then I don't have to ask anybody else."

"Good point." He gave her a nod and a gentle smile and added, "Enjoy your coffee." And he was gone.

She wasn't even sure she'd thanked him, and she needed to thank him for so many things. Not the least of which was giving her a second chance at their relationship. And she didn't even think he realized how much of a second chance he was giving her. Sure, he had said *Love you* in a text, but was it a friendly *love you* when she had been in the hospital, filled with worry, or was it more? Could it be more?

They hadn't talked about pursuing a relationship or their feelings or anything like that, but just knowing that she could be friends with him again was huge. And that he wasn't holding against her what she'd done before. She wasn't sure she would be quite so generous if their positions were reversed. She would like to think so, but lots of times in life she didn't think people were all that easy to get along with. She certainly hadn't been before, during her first rehab stint.

And now, after a much harder and slowly learned set of lessons, she knew that life had given her a whole lot more to think about. Not the least of which was what she would do with this second chance because that's what it felt like.

Coming back to Hathaway was part of that, like getting out of the hospital and being able to come back here, but also knowing that she was coming back here to Dennis.

And of course she was, whether he believed it or not. She was coming back here to Dennis. She smiled at that because she wasn't sure that he saw it, wasn't sure that he even realized how much she still cared about him.

"Or maybe he did at that," she muttered out loud. "How many other people would have come and brought me coffee, knowing that I was an early riser? Or would care about bringing me breakfast, as he is already planning to do?"

She wasn't so sure just how much they had left between them, but she had seen absolutely nothing so far to stop her from loving the man who she had always loved. She just hadn't realized that it was a true and lasting love that she couldn't live without, not until she had faced Dennis once more. Nothing like seeing a huge revelation in the light of day happen right in front of you, when you couldn't do anything about it.

BACK IN THE dining room at the buffet table, Dennis quickly worked his way through the morning, remembering to take her breakfast with a tray full of options on it. She picked out what she wanted, and he brought the rest back to the kitchen.

As he walked back into the kitchen again, Ilse smiled at him. "You make a great nursemaid."

He shrugged. "If I can be of service, I will do what I can," he declared cheerfully. "You know I don't care how or what, as long as someone needs help."

"And that makes you unique in this world," she said.

"I don't know about that," he countered. "I think a lot of people don't allow themselves to help others because they're always afraid of being judged as looking to get something in return. It's not about what you get in return. It's all about what you give, and people have forgotten that."

She smiled at him and gave him a gentle hug. "You're just a very fine person on the inside," she muttered. "And I've been very lucky to have you in my life." And, with that, she stepped away and answered her phone.

He stared at her, not sure what had brought that on. They'd always had a great working relationship, one he really appreciated. She was a wonderful cook, a wonderful person for that matter. And had come out of her shell more and more as time went on, partly because of her partner, Dennis was sure, but also just because Ilse felt more of a sense of personal satisfaction and had peace in her heart.

That also came when you found somebody you could spend your life with. Something that Dennis was still looking for and hoping that maybe a second chance with Yvonne was in the offing. Stan had given Dennis hope when Stan had had a second chance in his life with his previous girlfriend, and they too had been separated by space and time for years. Still, even the seemingly same circumstances were always different, and it never seemed to work out necessarily quite the way that one thought it would. Dennis could only hope to go down this pathway and just see where it went.

He worked his way through his day, checking in on Yvonne once again at lunchtime, but she was sleeping. Making a mental note to check on her later, he raced back down to the dining room to serve lunch to the other patients. By the time he was done, he realized that quite a bit of time had already passed.

He looked over at Dani, in line at his buffet table. "I checked on her earlier, but she was sleeping. Still, she probably needs lunch."

"And I checked on her just now," Dani shared. "She's still asleep."

He frowned. "I guess that's normal, *huh*?"

"It is, especially with the heavy antibiotics and the pain-killers after the surgery she's just come out of, yes," she explained. "The nurses are keeping a close eye on her."

He smiled. "Glad to hear that."

And, with that, he had to be content. By the time he had another break and a chance to go see her, he looked around the dining room and the kitchen to ensure that everything was taken care of at the moment, so that he could take off, only to find Ilse looking at him and waving him on.

"Go," she said. "You need to see if she's okay."

He nodded. "I do, but she's not all alone. The medical staff are looking after her."

Ilse just smiled and repeated, "Go."

And, with that, he gave her a broad grin and bolted. He hoped that this extra attention given to Yvonne wasn't affecting his work, but, of course, knowing that she was here and needed help with something, that would always weigh on him. Somehow, somewhere along the line, he needed to find a way to make peace with the fact that she was here but also that she was not his. Something he already knew, but he just didn't want to know. It was a conflict in his mind that he hadn't quite come to terms with.

When he knocked on her door gently the second time that afternoon, she called out to him to come in.

He opened the door and looked at her. "Hey, you're awake this time."

She nodded. "Yeah. I just woke up. I was looking for a nurse."

"I'll get you one," he offered. "I also wanted to see if you needed any lunch."

She frowned. "I'm not quite awake enough, so I don't think so."

"Okay. Let me call for a nurse. Meanwhile, I'm down at the kitchen. Ring me if you need me." She frowned at him. "I'm on your phone list as part of your team," he noted. And, with that, he was gone. He found her a nurse and then headed back to the kitchen.

Ilse looked up. "That was a fast visit."

"She just woke up and needed a nurse. She'll call me if she needs food."

"Good enough. You can wait for her to call, can't you?"

He winced. "I guess I seem pretty much like a love-struck teenager, *huh*?"

"Love-struck is not a bad thing," Ilse noted. "And you're nothing more than what you always have been, somebody who cares. In this case she probably just doesn't even realize how lucky she is that you do care."

"I don't know," he muttered, shrugging. "I don't even want to go down that pathway again."

"And yet, how can you not?" she asked. "It's obvious that you're still in love with her."

He froze at that and looked over at her. "It's that obvious, *huh*?"

She nodded. "Yes, it is. And it's nothing to be ashamed of either."

"Maybe not, but when that love was turned down the

first time," he admitted, with a heartfelt sigh, "it doesn't really make me feel any better to know that I'm still locked in the same time loop."

"Not the same time loop," she countered gently. "You're still in love with her, and she's still worthy of that love, and, just because time has passed, that doesn't mean the emotions have been eased."

"No, they haven't," he admitted, "and I'm still super excited to see her every day. And that doesn't say much for me."

"It doesn't say much for your happiness *if* she doesn't feel the same way about you as you do about her," she corrected, "but we do not know how she feels. Or do you?"

"No," he replied. "I haven't asked. Honestly, I've just been grateful that she's even in my life right now."

"And stick to that gratitude," Ilse suggested. "You know as well as I do how important it is."

He nodded. "I do know that. It's just hard, not knowing."

"Of course it is," she agreed. "In your mind you've loved and lost, and you don't want to get hurt again. But she's also loved and lost, and I think she's more afraid of hurting you this time around."

He stared at Ilse and then shrugged. "You could be right. I don't even begin to understand the vagaries of all this."

"Of course not," she teased. "Nothing is quite so hard to fathom as love."

"Love, and love you've lost," he added. "It definitely feels as if I've lost something."

"And maybe it was just a step she needed to take in the past, but now she's back again and wiser for having had her *life in the world* experience."

"I could hope so," he murmured, "but ..." And then he didn't say anything more. When he looked up, not too long later, he saw the same nurse approaching him.

"Hey, she's asking for you, if you've got a moment," she shared.

"She's looking for food?" he asked immediately, looking down at the leftovers he was putting away. "You know what she would like?"

"No, I don't. She didn't mention food, just wants to speak with you."

He froze and looked up at her. "Did she say ... anything?" He hesitated.

The nurse, who hadn't been here long and probably didn't know any of his history with Yvonne, shook her head. "No, I just told her that I would pass on the message."

"Thank you." He looked over at Ilse, who nodded at him.

"Go," she urged. "You know you don't have to ask."

He shrugged, wondering if he should go right away. Yet he knew he would be completely useless until he figured this out. He was soon walking at a fast clip to her room. When he got there, he knocked on the door and poked his head around the door that opened under his fingers. "Hey, you okay?" he called out. He watched as she slowly came out of the bathroom, saw him, and smiled.

"Hey," she greeted him.

"You're up and moving," he noted. "That's good."

"Well, I'm up, and I guess I'm moving," she quipped. "Can't say it feels as if I'm moving very well though."

He shook his head and smiled. "You're moving after having some touch-and-go surgery," he pointed out, "so that's a wonderful start." She slowly made her way back to her bed, and he noted the pain on her face. "I wasn't sure if you were looking for lunch yet," he noted.

"I don't know that I can eat lunch at the moment. I need the painkiller to kick in."

"Right," he replied, feeling foolish because he'd not even considered that.

She waved a hand at him. "That doesn't mean I wouldn't take another cup of coffee though."

"Good. Coming right up," he stated and closed her door and bolted to the dining room. There he poured her some coffee, thought about it and reached for a small meat pie off to the side, left over from lunch. He put that on a plate and brought both back to her.

She eyed the meat pie, as she sat in her visitor's chair. "I might just manage that much."

"Well, you might. I'm not trying to push it. I just thought maybe it would ease the coffee in case that started to upset your stomach. Plus, some of these pills are pretty rough on the stomach, and sometimes food helps."

"The nurse told me that I could eat. I just didn't think that I wanted to yet. Not until the painkiller kicked in."

"Did you want help getting back into bed?" he asked, worried that she was pale, exhausted-looking.

"Honestly, … I would really love to get out and around for a little bit, but I probably shouldn't start that yet."

"What do you mean?" he asked.

"I was just thinking that, if I was stronger, I could wheel myself down and go out to the gardens."

He shook his head immediately. "Oh no you don't. That's definitely taking it too far."

She nodded. "I know. You're right." She looked up at him hopefully. "Don't suppose you have a half an hour, do you?"

"For what?" he asked, looking around.

She smiled. "To take me out to the gardens."

He stared at her in shock. "Maybe, if you think it's okay to be sitting up that long?" he replied hesitantly.

"Oh, I shouldn't even be asking. I know that you're crazy busy at work."

"Yeah, it's always busy at work. You know that."

"I do know that, so don't worry about it."

"If you don't think that'll put too much strain on your body, I do have some time." Mentally he calculated in his head what he needed to finish. "I can go complete a few things," he explained, "and then I can take you outside."

She looked at him hopefully. "Do you mind?"

"No, of course not. I'll do a few things in the kitchen and be right back."

"That sounds good," she said, "because I'll have my coffee and potentially get rid of this pain while you're doing your thing."

And, with that, he returned to work, a smile on his face and hope in his heart for the first time in a very long time.

Chapter 10

YVONNE RUBBED HER sore temple, knowing she should probably not even be encouraging a relationship between the two of them because everything hurt—but most of all her heart, her whole chest. It was as if she'd been beaten up pretty roughly, and, of course, she had definitely had some surgery done, with people poking around in her insides. So some healing still had to happen, but it felt pretty much the same way it had before she went into surgery. Yet it did seem to lessen each day. Was she just hopeful or was that her new reality?

Her surgeon had warned her about that, saying recovery wouldn't happen overnight. It was just such a weird feeling. But every time she saw Dennis, she just wanted to spend time with him, more time than she by rights could pull from him. He had to spend time here with his job, while she was the one who basically was taking up time. She sighed heavily as she thought about it.

"Is there any fool like an old fool," she muttered to herself. At that, she heard a chuckle and looked up to see Dani.

"Hey." Dani smiled, then asked, "You okay?"

"I am. I'm waiting for the painkillers to kick in. And I think I've convinced Dennis to take half an hour and push me around the gardens."

"Good," Dani noted. "It would be good for you."

"But it wouldn't be good for the two of us?" Yvonne asked in a wry tone. "I feel as if I shouldn't even be going in this direction."

"Why is that?" Dani asked, bringing her a bunch of paperwork.

Yvonne looked at the paperwork and sighed. "Hopefully this is all good stuff."

"It is. I just need signatures," Dani replied cheerfully.

And, with that, Yvonne signed the paperwork.

Dani stepped back and added, "You still didn't tell me why you're afraid this isn't a good move."

"I just feel like, what if what we had before isn't still there, and what if something is still there, but we want different things now?"

"Sounds to me as if you're worrying about something that you can't even begin to worry about yet," she suggested.

"Maybe, but it feels odd."

"Sure, you're opening a door that you closed," Dani pointed out. "So don't open it if you want it to stay closed. However, if you're not sure what you want or if you're thinking that maybe you want to see what's there or what's potentially still available between you two, then that's a door you must open to find out more." And, with that, Dani was gone.

As she contemplated Dani's words, Yvonne slowly ate the meat pie, marveling at how the kitchen here always put out food that was tasty and simple and yet hit the palate. By the time she was done and her coffee was gone, she was tired again. And that wasn't good because she'd already mentioned going outside with Dennis. But only so much she could do about the fatigue hitting her, along with the painkiller.

She closed her eyes, hoping Dennis would take a little

bit longer to look after whatever he had to finish, and just curled up on the side of her bed. She didn't use a blanket, just snuggled in and closed her eyes for a minute, just, … just a couple minutes to let the fatigue take over. She heard an odd noise to her side, and she woke up with a start, bolted upright, and then cried out in pain.

Almost immediately Dennis was there, his hands on her shoulders, whispering, "Easy, take it easy. I didn't mean to wake you."

She groaned as she laid back on her bed, her shoulder now killing her. "It's okay. I just wanted to close my eyes for a minute," she murmured. "But of course that minute turned into a lot of minutes, courtesy of that painkiller."

"And that's what you're here for," he reminded her. "You're here to heal."

She nodded. "But I really wanted to go outside."

"How do you feel now about going outside?" he asked, studying her carefully. "Do you think you're up for it, or will it be too much?"

"Well, if I'm not doing the work to move the wheelchair," she noted, "it won't be too much to just sit there."

"But you don't know that until you've tried it," Dennis stated. "I guess if we take it slow and easy …"

"Absolutely," she agreed. "If nothing else, it'll be a good change of scenery for me."

"We'll see." Dennis brought over the wheelchair for her. "Can you get into this without hurting yourself?"

"It seems as if everything I do hurts me these days," she murmured. "One way or another, at least." He frowned at her, but she left her cryptic comment hanging in the air and didn't want to even discuss it. She just smiled and added, "I'm fine."

He frowned back at her. "You don't sound fine."

"I am, just surgery is never the easiest."

"No, it definitely isn't, particularly this one. But the good news is, the surgery solved a long-term problem for you."

"I hope so. I wasn't thinking that it would be this long of a recovery."

He burst out laughing. "What are you talking about? It's just been a few days."

"They went in microscopically," she pointed out. "It's not as if they put a six-inch slash in my back."

"I'm sure your back doesn't care to have the new wound measured either," he said, with spirit. "As far as your body is concerned, it's been damaged and hurt and invaded, and any attempt to minimize that agony won't go over well for a while."

She just smiled at him. "You could be right." Once she was sitting in the wheelchair, she looked over at him. "You okay to push?"

"Of course I am. I lift huge sacks of flour on a regular basis," he shared. "I'm not exactly a weakling."

"I didn't mean it that way," she replied. "I just meant, are you okay to … to do this, with me?"

"Yes, of course. Now let's do this."

And, with that, she closed her mouth and let him take her outside.

DENNIS WASN'T EXACTLY sure where her odd mood was coming from, but it was starting to set off his mood too. As soon as he got her outside to the beautiful grounds, she sighed happily.

"This is what I was missing," she whispered.

"And what is that?" he asked.

"Fresh air, Mother Nature. Just a chance to be out here. No pressure, no stress, just life."

"And this can happen every day for you," he suggested. "We're all about figuring out just what you need and getting it for you. It all aids in healing."

She nodded. "Last time at rehab, I got outside by myself, but now I'm working at asking people to help me get what I need," she admitted, with a small smile.

"And I think you're doing very well," he noted.

She looked at him. "In what way?" she asked.

"Well, you asked to go outside. You asked for breakfast. You asked for lunch and coffee," he explained. "For you, those are huge milestones. In the past, you would have said, *No, I'll do without coffee because I can't get down there myself.* There's been many times that you made it to mealtimes very late. Still, I knew you were coming, so I was still holding back food for you. If you got there too late, you wouldn't get anything hot to eat. So I stayed open much longer to try and give you a chance to get down there, with that stubborn pride of yours."

Her breath rushed out of her in a gasp. "Wow, I had no idea."

"Of course not. I never told you." He smiled as he pushed her onto the pathway and down toward the horses.

"How come so many horses are here?" She gasped. "I just realized that Midnight's here."

"I think at the moment we have six."

"And a llama too. Wow, Dani's really collecting strays, isn't she?"

"I don't think she looks at it as collecting strays as much as she likes to consider herself helping animals in need," he clarified.

"And that's much more appropriate, isn't it? She told me that her husband's coming to work with Stan. Well, her future husband is," she corrected.

"Exactly, and that'll happen faster than we expect too," he shared. "We're working on her menu planning for the wedding."

She laughed. "She did tell me about it. She's a little chagrined to think that everybody is pitching in for this."

"Of course she is, because Dani cares, and she wants the money to go to the center, but it's also good for everybody here to see her take the next big step in her life." He chuckled. "Besides, we can do this blindfolded. She's just afraid it's taking us away from the regular work."

"Which it would never do," Yvonne interjected.

"No, it never would," he confirmed, with a smile.

"She's worried because she knows it's eating into your personal time. Still, it's interesting to watch her be almost that nervous schoolgirl over the whole thing," Yvonne said, with a smile.

"Well, it's a big step for her, and she's waited a long time."

"She also brought up an interesting thing about that. She looks back on how long they waited, and she wished they had just gotten married right away, instead of all this production that now waits for her and all the time that they lost when they could have been together."

"Interesting," he murmured, his mind racing to the times that he'd seen her both sad and lonely. "And I can see that. Ever since they first met again—after all, they knew each other growing up—but there was always a part of her missing."

"Yes, I think she would agree with that," Yvonne replied. "So I'm glad that the wedding is happening soon. I think she feels as if she spent more than enough time alone."

"I'm sure she has. You obviously spent a lot of time talking to Dani."

"It was on the drive home from the hospital," Yvonne explained. "It really makes her human in that we forget she's got her own life on hold for so much of this as well."

"It's on hold, but I think it's been something that she's been okay with, at least on the short term. Obviously she's delighted that the waiting period is coming to an end, but then we all are." He nodded. "We're all looking forward to the wedding."

Yvonne sighed. "I don't know if I'll still be here or not, but it would be nice to come for the wedding."

"Then come," he said immediately.

"I can't just gate-crash if I'm not a patient here," she replied, laughing. "And I'm pretty sure you already have more than enough people to feed, and her wedding won't be something that she extends any more invitations to."

"We are all invited. All of the staff are welcome to come, plus one," he stated. "So, if you want, feel free to come as my plus one."

Yvonne didn't seem to know what to say. She stared up at him in shock.

But not hearing a yes blurting right from her mouth, he realized that either the shock was too great or it wouldn't be an answer that he wanted to hear. He turned her around and added, "Think about it. You don't have to give me your answer now." He feigned a cheerful tone.

Chapter 11

Y ET SHE REALIZED that, by not giving him an instant yes, a *she would be delighted* response, she'd hurt him yet again. "It's definitely not a no. You just really surprised me."

"Of course I did, not to mention I'm not exactly subtle."

"You are as you always are, honest and straightforward."

"Which isn't necessarily what people want. I get it."

"No, you don't get it," she said in exasperation. "You literally just shocked me. I wasn't even thinking that going was possible."

He didn't say anything, just continued to push her slowly back toward the main building.

"I don't know if she would take my attendance kindly though," Yvonne muttered.

"Why not?" he asked curiously. "Do you think Dani minds?"

"I don't know how Dani feels about it. I know that I would feel guilty."

"Going to her wedding?" he asked in astonishment.

"Going as your plus one, if I wasn't your plus one," she pointed out.

At that, Dennis slowed her wheelchair. "Ah. Okay. I guess from your point of view that's probably something you don't want anything to do with, so that's fine. It was just a thought. Don't get upset about it."

As they got closer to the building, she felt the distance between them widening. "I don't know what I think at the moment, so maybe you could leave your invitation open?" She couldn't see his face, but she waited for his reply.

"Of course."

She smiled and added, "Thanks. I haven't been a very fast learner in life," she admitted. "I am trying to get better."

"You're fast enough," he said.

Yet an odd note filled his tone that she didn't really understand. "No, I don't think I am. I think I've hurt a lot of people because I was so determined to be independent that I forgot about just being me."

"That's an interesting comment," he said. "I thought you prided yourself on being you."

"Yeah, and I think I forgot who that was. … I think it was caught up in medical bills and surgeries and recoveries and rehab and trying to be what everybody else wanted me to be," she murmured. "I forgot who I actually am. Being here, back at Hathaway, is helping me to remember."

"And yet would you say you were *you* back then?" he asked curiously.

"I thought I was, but I don't think I was in a way. I feel as if I took a wrong turn somewhere, and that wrong turn took me down a pathway that, sure, I probably needed to go on, but it wasn't a pathway that I see now as one that I would choose to take."

"That's a little confusing."

"No, it goes back to the hindsight stuff," she muttered, with a heavy sigh. "If I could have avoided so much in my life, I would have. But it really feels as if I'm here to relearn something, something important."

"When you figure it out," Dennis shared, "you know all of us will be interested in seeing and hearing about it, if you're ready to share." He seemed to backtrack for a bit. "We're all here for you."

She nodded at that. "And I do know that. Thank you."

AFTER SETTLING YVONNE back in her room, Dennis returned to the kitchen, quiet, as he contemplated everything that she'd said.

"Hey," Ilse greeted him. "You okay?"

He nodded. "Yeah. She just mentioned a couple things to me today that helped me to understand where she's at and why she's so confused—yet it's not really a help."

"No, a lot of that stuff never is helpful to anybody else but the person trying to figure out things themselves. And I'm not surprised if she feels as if this is a second chance, or in some way that she took a wrong turn somewhere. I felt that way in my life too. I'm sure Dani has too. I'm sure all of us have in some ways. And this may be Yvonne's chance to get it right this time. But, by that same token, she probably feels a lot of pressure to get it right, and, if she doesn't understand this time, then how to get it right will be an added stress."

He groaned. "Does everybody automatically do things, or think things, or create situations where they're stressed to the max?" he asked. "It just seems as if life should be simple, and yet it's not."

"It's simple for people who have it figured out or who come from the heart 100 percent of the time, where there is much less to figure out," she pointed out, looking over at him. "But not everybody has the ability to decide what the right path forward is. You made a decision a long time ago, and it put her on a different path because I think she—honestly, I think she regrets it. I think she regrets turning you down."

Dennis shook his head. "I think she's back because she had an accident, and she needs to heal again," he declared. "When I offered to take her to Dani's wedding as my plus one today, it threw her completely, and she was looking for a way to say no."

"*Was* she looking for a way to say no?" Ilse asked. "Or was she just looking for an answer that was honest inside herself? You probably completely sprung it on her, so she had absolutely no idea what to say. Then, when she didn't respond fast enough, you would've taken it as an immediate no."

"She did ask me to keep the invitation open," he admitted, "saying that I had surprised her. And I did take it as a no, and she didn't necessarily let me off the hook on that either," he stated, with a laugh.

"Good, somebody needs to jolt you out of your own complacency sometimes too."

"Is that what I am?" he asked, looking over at her, startled.

"You're very secure, Dennis. That is incredibly healthy," she murmured. "It's also, for a lot of people, incredibly unnerving."

He stared at her, completely flummoxed.

She smiled. "And even just the fact that you don't understand why or how something like that could happen is great, but not everybody comes from a position where they know who they are. I think, in Yvonne's case, she tried hard to find out who she was over these last five years. Either she doesn't like the result or realized that who she is isn't the person who she was pretending to be."

"That … kind of makes sense to me."

"That's good," Ilse replied, "but don't go telling her that."

He burst out laughing. "No, I won't. I love her too much for that."

At his wording she stopped to consider him. "Still?"

He nodded. "Yes. Still."

"Well. that's a good thing, and, as long as you have some forgiveness in your heart, then maybe you'll get there yet."

"I don't need to forgive her," he countered. "When I said I loved her way back when and even now, that didn't come with a catch. It didn't come with an expiration date. It didn't come with conditions, *I'll love you only if,*" he shared. "I meant it. I love her. All and completely."

Ilse smiled mistily. "You're one of the good guys, and it always surprises me when I hear something like that coming from you because I know you mean it. I know that you believe it and that so many good things out there are waiting for you. However, I just don't think Yvonne necessarily understands that. And having somebody in her world that is so self-confident about who he is, where he wants to go, who he wants to share his life with, and what he wants to do, I'm sure is incredibly unnerving for her."

"Maybe unnerving, sure. But is that something I should avoid?" he asked. "I mean, is it something I need to change?"

"No," she said immediately. "That would be sad for all of us if you did. You come from the heart in a way that most of us can't even begin to imagine. The self-confidence that you exude is healthy, it's healing, and it's beautiful," she added. "We all feel love coming from you. All of us, me, the rest of the staff, Dani, we all want you in our corner in life," she murmured, with a smile in his direction.

"I think you just need to give Yvonne time to assimilate. Remember that these veterans are wounded, and their self-esteem and their self-identity has taken a hit. It may take her healing before her own confidence returns."

Dennis eyed Ilse, then nodded slowly. "I was thinking time might be, in this case, one of the best things I could do for her. Yet I will admit it's hard to wait." He shook his head. "I just want to wrap her up and to make everything right in her world."

"And yet you can't do that," she replied. "*Yvonne* has to make everything right in her world. There are times when we can do everything for others and then times when we can do nothing, and it's up to them to do what's required," she explained. "This is one of those times."

Chapter 12

FOR SEVERAL DAYS Yvonne pondered and wrote in a journal and pondered some more.

When Shane popped into her room and asked, "Hey, how are you doing, and how are you feeling about possibly going back to work?"

She smiled at him. "Well, unbeknownst to you, I have been working." And she lifted up her journal.

"Ah, that's the work that you need to do as well," he agreed. "I was wondering more about the physical."

"If you say I'm ready, then I'm ready to give rehab a shot."

"As long as you listen to your body," he reminded her. "No going too strong, too hard, or trying to improve on things that can't be improved on right now," he stated. "You have to stop, if and when it gets to be too much."

"Right. And I guess I wasn't very good at that before, was I?"

"It doesn't matter what you were or you weren't before," he stated, with a look in her direction, "because you are who you are now. Remember that, and it's all good."

She stopped and stared at him. "What did you just say?"

He frowned at her. "I'm saying that you can't always look behind you. You have to look in front of you. The person you were five years ago is not the person you are today. So whatever the person you used to be doesn't apply today. Therefore, don't be carrying those kinds of thoughts forward because they don't apply anymore. If it was still you from back then, sure, I would tell you to ease back and to remember that you have to listen to your body and do all the rest of that stuff, but you're not that person."

He smiled gently. "Even so, will I tell you the same thing? Sure, for some areas, but with a completely different attitude, knowing that you already know your body's been through a mess. You are well aware that your body needs to catch a break right now. So, as soon as it's painful, you'll tell me that. I'm trusting that you'll do that because I see the person you are today."

He smacked the doorframe gently and asked, "Twenty minutes and down to PT?" When she gave a dazed nod, he smiled. "Good. See you then." And he left.

She was absolutely flabbergasted by the insights everybody in this place provided, which was astronomical. Only as she wheeled her way toward Shane's big therapy center did she wonder whether she had missed it all last time or hadn't been quite there mentally, or been ready, or whatever the deal was for taking in all these lessons. She should have picked up some of them the last time and yet didn't. All that wisdom and life experience had just passed her by.

When she rejoined Shane, she began, "What you just said back there."

"*Uh-huh*," he muttered, staring down at his computer monitor. "What about it?"

"Was I completely oblivious last time?" she asked.

He looked at her and then shrugged. "Oblivious, no. Were you directed in a completely different way? Yes. Were you dedicated, driven to be somebody? Absolutely."

"Was that wrong?"

"No, don't even think that way," he stated, with a smile. "Yet it's obvious you're a very different person today."

"I can't argue that," she conceded. "I feel very different."

"After the surgery, how do you feel?"

"Almost like I have a new lease on life. That was a gift I didn't realize I needed."

"Oh good, because it was, it was a huge gift. And the fact that your body gave that to you and that you came through it with flying colors is also huge," he said, with a bright smile. "Now I'll start very easy, and remember what I told you."

She nodded. "Don't worry. I have no intention of dealing with pain this time around."

"Good." And, with that, they got started.

DENNIS WALKED DOWN the hallway toward the end of the day. He was tired but wondering whether Yvonne wanted to have dinner together or already had plans, or just what her thought processes were. He wanted to give her time, but he also didn't want to give her so much time that it ran away on them. Plus, he found her getting closer to other people. He didn't really want to hold her back because everybody needed friends, everybody needed somebody on this rehab journey with them. He'd seen it happen time and time again, and he wanted that for her, if she was in a position to accept it for herself.

Something else that would be good would be if they could talk about things, just to let her know that that was potentially something she might want to cultivate. He didn't know how she felt about those things, and given the chance to talk hadn't been as abundant as he had hoped. Still, he didn't want to push any conversations on her that would strain their time together. When he knocked on her door, she gave a very tired answer. Frowning, he poked his head around the door, took one look at her, and said, "Ouch."

She nodded. "*Ouch* is right. I promised I wouldn't do very much, and I didn't do very much," she explained. "I did listen to my body, and I did tell Shane when to stop," she shared. "Yet I'm sitting here, realizing how little I can do and how far I really have to go to be where I need to be." When he went to say something, she held up a hand. "No, I'm not complaining. It's just a fact of life that I do have a long way to go this time. I did last time as well, but it just feels so much bigger now."

"It probably is, because you're carrying old injuries along with new injuries. And I'm sorry that reality has to be such a real downer."

She nodded. "It definitely is a real downer." She smiled at him. "And why are you here?"

"Because I'm off shift more or less for a little bit, and then it'll be dinnertime. I wondered how your day had been and whether you wanted to go for dinner tonight."

"If I go to dinner with you tonight, I have to go later."

He nodded. "So we have an option of having coffee or an ice cream, something light right now, and then something bigger and more filling later. I might need to eat before the dinner rush though."

She frowned at that. "I'm not hungry yet. Honestly, my stomach still feels kind of sick from the workout I did with Shane. And, yes, I know. ... I didn't think I overdid it," she muttered. "Honestly, I really tried hard *not* to overdo it, but wow."

He nodded. "Even learning where your body's capabilities stop and start is huge. This is a whole new journey for you. In your head, it's probably like this is your second time round, how this is your second rodeo. So, it should be something you already know, and you already can do," he pointed out. "However, I think your body's telling you that everything's different this time."

"*Everything*," she agreed, with emphasis, "is different. It's as if I was sleepwalking last time. I was in some weird zone, where I was just focused on point A, and everything else was secondary." She shook her head. "I honestly don't even know what to say about some of it, but it was pretty amazing in many ways and pretty shocking now that I look back on it."

"And again you can't just look back on everything," he murmured.

She smiled and nodded. "Shane said something about that today that was really profound."

He waited, wondering what insights Shane had come up with.

"He mentioned something about how I can't look in the rearview mirror or I can't look behind me all the time. I have to stop and look forward. And he won't look behind. He won't even consider the person I was before when it comes to my attitude, my training, the way I react to injuries or to him, to telling him this is too much or this isn't enough. Because, as he says it, I'm not that person. So he's treating me like a completely new person who will do what is necessary to get back on her feet, but at a pace that's comfortable and sensible because that's what he would want for me. And he's expecting me to fall in line and to do it that way."

"And what was your reaction to that?" Dennis asked curiously. Mentally he wanted to go high-five Shane.

"I had this great big, almost earth-shattering awareness that the person I was doesn't have to be part of who I am today," she admitted, looking over at him with a smile. "And I know that sounds like a cop-out, and I don't mean it that way, but I'm still working my way through everything he, … he stirred up. It's not as if he upset me, so that's definitely not part of it. It's just, it comes back to the fact that so many insights into life and character can be found here that sometimes it stuns me when I hear it said out loud. It just hits that spot, and it opens things up in a way that I never understood before."

"Sounds as if you really needed to hear that from Shane then," Dennis stated, with a delighted smile.

She stared at him for a long moment. "I really needed to hear that. And I suspect it'll be a few days before I even understand the ramifications of what he did say."

"And maybe quite a bit longer," he said. "When you get one of those big shifts in understanding, I think it's, …it's not even something that you really understand the full implications of within those first few days. Sometimes I think it's potentially weeks to months."

She nodded slowly. "I think you're right. And every-thing, *everything*, feels different this time around." She shook her head. "And I, … I would not have believed it if some-body had told me that ahead of time."

"It's a good thing nobody did then," he teased. "And what do you want to do about food? And, if you need to stay here and just contemplate Shane's words, that's okay too."

She smiled at him. "I forgot just how easy to get along with you are. Sometimes it's almost too easy, and I feel as if

I'm taking advantage."

He stared at her in astonishment. "You're not taking advantage. I'm happy, happy to be a part of this journey, happy to watch you explore, learn, change, grow," he shared. "Whatever it is that you need to be doing, I'm happy to be witnessing your growth. As you grow and change, so do I. So does everybody here. … I would like to think it's a collective consciousness, where one person learns, and another person learns because of that person's learning. Little bits and pieces of us fly through. For another person to see you succeed might give them the motivation to achieve a little bit of success in their own world," he murmured.

"I'm not trying to be metaphysical or spiritual or any-thing else. I just think that, when so many people are on board in a place like this, it's important that everybody look around and see the progress that everybody else is making and take to heart what they can use for themselves."

"And you're right, of course. You're right." She laughed. "I don't think I've ever known you guys *not* to be right."

"Oh, yes," he replied, flashing her a grin. "It happens, and it happens a lot, but we do our best."

She nodded. "So what about that ice cream?"

He laughed out loud. He grabbed her wheelchair, twist-ed it around, and said, "Your chauffeur, ma'am."

"You mean, my car or my limousine or my carriage. Hey, I like that better. How about my carriage?"

"Or a pumpkin," he suggested.

She burst out laughing. "Lord, I do remember that sense of rapport," she muttered, with a happy sigh. "That sense of laughter and light, that sense of not being judged. I don't know where that judgment in my own head came from," she noted, shaking her head. "It seems so wrong now."

"And yet, back then maybe it wasn't wrong. Maybe it's what you needed. Maybe going this pathway, however convoluted it may seem to you right now," he suggested, "maybe it's the right pathway for you."

"I certainly think that sometimes we aren't privy to what's right and wrong because we get to make decisions. So we get to make things right or wrong in our heads. Sometimes we get a chance to redo something so that it's better or it's more aligned with who we are now, and that would fit me too," she admitted, as she slowly made her way into the wheelchair, sagging into the seat with relief. "It's such a relief to have a wheelchair and to not have to push it myself. What is it about needing to be nurtured?"

"I think it's acknowledging that this is a low spot physically for you in life, and that you need help, and, while you're here, lots of people will help you," he declared. "So, take advantage of that, make it something that's yours, and do it knowing it won't be forever."

He wheeled her out of her room and down to the kitchen. "Now, we talked about ice cream. Do you need solid food first?"

She shook her head. "No, I definitely think ice cream would be the choice right now, and, if you've got a moment, maybe enjoy it with me out on the deck?"

"Sure, I've got a few minutes. I can't stay for too long, but I've got a little bit of time." She nodded. "And, of course, I have to go get the ice cream," he added. "What flavor do you want?"

"I don't mind. Bring me whatever."

And, with a smile, he dashed into the back of the kitchen. She sat here in the middle of the dining room, waiting for him.

Chapter 13

YVONNE SAT IN the dining room for a long moment, waiting for Dennis. When he reappeared with two large cones, she gasped. "I guess I won't need much dinner."

"You will," he stated cheerfully. "And, whenever you're ready, don't forget to ask Shane for permission to get into the pool."

"I haven't yet. I'm not quite there."

"I get that, and I don't even know with your incision whether you're allowed into the pool yet, with all its chemicals."

"No, I'm not, but I want to swim, as soon as I'm cleared for it," she murmured. "I do remember that part last time. It was pretty nice. Do you go in often?"

He shook his head. "Nope, I don't."

"Not since, *huh*?"

He looked over at her, gave her a gentle smile, and replied, "No, not *since*."

Her shoulders sagged. "You used to love it."

"Yep, I did, and then that changed."

"Right," she murmured, "because of me."

"If it was because of you," he noted, "it's because I let that happen. You are not responsible for taking something away from me."

She looked at him and then winced. "You figured that

out already, *huh?*"

"I did," he confirmed, with a chuckle.

"Right." She sighed. "I am looking forward to getting back into the pool when I get a chance."

"And maybe I'll join you," he said, as he stared down at his ice cream. "Maybe I will. I'll see. Not tonight though," he murmured. "I've still got dinner to serve."

"Hey, you promised me food," she reminded him in a teasing voice.

"And I fully intend to honor that promise," he declared, with a big smile in her direction. "But you can bet an awful lot of people are looking for food first."

"Once they figure out that I got an ice cream to tide me over, how do you think they'll feel?"

"They'll feel the same way they always do, when they see somebody sneaking around the halls with ice cream. That they lost out." Dennis chuckled. "And some days it's just fun to give everybody something special," he stated, with a smile. "Hathaway House is a very special place to work, and even to rehab in."

"And after all these years you're still happy here, aren't you?"

He nodded. "Absolutely," he stated, with a smile. "I can't imagine being anyplace else."

"And I guess that was the thing that I didn't understand back then," she admitted. "It seemed as if you had no ambition, and you had no need to go anywhere, as if you settled for less." He stared at her in shock, and she shrugged. "That was the person I was back then."

His grin flashed at her honest clarification.

"It's not who I am now," she added, "and I'm sorry that I was that person back then because I don't think she understood very much about what was important to you."

"A lot of things are important to me, but, five years ago, it was more about you getting what you needed out of this place," he murmured. "And this time you seem to be seeking a completely different rehab experience."

Yvonne laughed. "This time at Hathaway House is so very different for me. And I can also see what you do and how you do it makes you such a necessary part of Hathaway House. You're really part of the heart and soul of this community," she shared, "and I didn't, … I didn't see that before. I didn't realize that the Dennis I knew and cared so much about was somebody everybody else cared about too." She paused, frowning. "I couldn't see that back then. I couldn't see what you gave the community as a whole. How sad."

"Not sad at all," he countered. "I wasn't there to, … to show off or to be a big conspicuous part of anything," he explained. "I was—I was just being true to me."

She looked over at him, her heart swelling, and she nodded. "You see? That's the thing. You're just being you, and, by being you, you have brought so much to the table, to the people here. Yet I just couldn't see it before. I couldn't see the value in that because it didn't make you money, it didn't make you a big name, it didn't make you puff up every morning and look in the mirror and say, *Yes, I've made it.*"

"Why would I want to do that?" he asked in astonishment. She stared at him and then started to laugh. By the time she finally slowed down, he repeated his question. "Okay, so something was funny to you when I asked you *why*, but I do want to understand this. Why would I want to do that?"

She sighed, more serious now. "Because, in my case, I

needed to do all that—make big money, make a big name for myself in my chosen industry, and declare in the mirror each morning how I had truly made it. Those were my external milestones that proved how I had created my new world to my standards, how I had succeeded. Yet you don't need to do that because you already know on the inside that what you do brings so much value that it would break everybody's heart here if you left." She shrugged. "I didn't have that sense of confidence, that sense of self." She faced him and stated, "You did, and you do, and it's perfect."

DENNIS STARED AT her in shock. "Oh, wow. I can't think of anybody ever saying anything so nice to me," he murmured. "It's, ... it's lovely that you said that, but don't in any way think that it makes you less than who you are."

She smiled. "I know who I am now. Five years ago I was somebody who thought I was so much less, and I needed to do so much more in order to build myself up," she explained. "I'm not that person anymore. And, if ever I needed that reminder, it was to come here this time around. ... I really did take a strange step to the left, and this really is a *coming home* moment for me. And, even though I know I have a good five, six months of grueling rehab ahead for me, it is so good to be here." She looked up at him. "And honestly, of all the things that I missed the most, it was you."

He stared at her, and then crouched in front of her, grabbed her hands with his, and whispered, "I missed you too, but I also knew that I had to let you go."

She smiled. "That's because you were wiser than I was."

"No, I haven't been through the trauma you have." He

shook his head. "I didn't get knocked off my path. I didn't get knocked off my feet, and I didn't get jolted into finding another way to make a living or how to go forward in life. Life for me has been easy. It's been smooth, and I could do my best at a job without too much stress because I didn't have too much conflict. Being here is a joy, a gift, and I love it." He shrugged.

"I understand that not everybody agrees with me, especially when we focus on my career path. I understand that, for some people, they want to be doctors and surgeons and firefighters and God-only-knows whatever else people want to do, but that's good for them. It's not for me though. It's not what I want. It's not who I am, and, for this point in time in my life, being here, helping all the patients, bringing them joy," he described, "is one of the best things I can do."

She nodded. "You're right."

He placed a finger against her lips. "I wish we had talked earlier, all those years ago, because I probably never told you," he shared, "how much I admire everything that you have done, everything you have handled. It's easy for people on the outside to tell you that you need to do more or to work harder or to change your exercises, but we aren't the ones with the broken bodies. We aren't the ones with shattered emotions, with nightmares that steal our sleep from us, that steal the dreams that you had for yourself," he murmured, gently rubbing his thumb against her chin. "We haven't been tested the way you have been, and not just once but now twice," he added.

She felt the tears gather in her eyes as she whispered, "It's been really tough."

He nodded. "I could say, *Yes, it's been tough, and I understand*, but, of course, I can't understand," he admitted. "I don't know what it's like to lose a leg, to lose an arm, to lose whatever body parts. I think all lost body parts probably require a grieving process. I haven't had any of those trials. You've had a trial by fire over and over again. And you have handled it with aplomb. You've handled it with as much gumption as anybody I have met.

"However, this time in rehab, you say that you lost your chutzpa. Maybe. But maybe it's more a case of an acceptance of life, an acceptance of where you're at right now. And that's okay too. Still, you do need to go easy on yourself and to realize that you have done so much, and you have done it all with your head high, and you've done it your way.

"So I'm not telling you to do anything my way. I don't know what's best for you. I can only tell you what I would like to see is what is best for the two of us, but I won't push that. I won't push anything." He nodded. "You're here for several months. I want you to enjoy it. I want you to find joy in your heart as much as you can and as long as you can, knowing that you're on a pathway that works for you, knowing that you can do this."

She smiled. "I do know I can do it because I have done it before. Yet I want you to know that my plans this time around are to do it in a very different way," she began. "I plan to relax. I plan to rest. I plan to enjoy every day. I plan to wake up and to smile because I had a chance to wake up. ... It felt last time as if I needed to make the most of every waking moment, and it was a frantic pace, but I, ... I couldn't for the life of me slow down."

He nodded. "And we saw that. We knew that, but we couldn't find a way to get you to understand that it needed to change."

"Well, life found a way. I got stopped with that last accident. And this time, I want to listen to the warnings. I want to listen to the advice. I want to take my time to do it right. I didn't want to come back here, and yet I love it here. It is home for me, and it's a stupid thing to say, but it feels as if I'm coming home. It's not just about the place. I know what it is. I know why it is. I just hadn't expected it to happen again," she murmured.

He frowned at her.

She smiled and shrugged. "We don't have to talk about this now. I know you have to go to work, so we'll postpone some of this discussion for later."

"Only if you want to," he replied, looking as if he wanted to say something more. And, indeed, he did. He wanted to say so much more, yet he didn't want to push her.

"Why don't we meet after dinner?" she asked. "And then we can talk some more."

He nodded. "That sounds good to me. I have a meeting to discuss Dani's wedding feast, but, as soon as that's done, I'll call you. How's that?"

"Sounds good, and you might even find me sitting out on the deck anyway."

"Good. I like the sound of that. Now let's get you back up where you belong." And, with her tucked back into her room, Dennis headed down to the dining area for the rest of his workday.

By the time dinner came and went, he was still on a high from his conversation with Yvonne. Nobody had mentioned anything about how he was beaming, but lots of discreet smiles had been shared among the staff, and Dennis was fine with that. He was so okay with that. It was way better than the commiserating looks of somebody whose love was not returned that he'd gone through last time. And, even back then, he'd known it wasn't the end of the Chapter.

He'd just known that the Chapter with Yvonne had taken a turn he didn't expect. And now here he was, hopeful that there would be some exchange that would make him absolutely ecstatic, but he was really hesitant to hurry down that pathway too far, just in case she still wasn't ready. And he didn't know what she was ready for at this stage either. Just because he wanted her to be ready for something more didn't mean she would be.

Ilse asked, "You okay for the meeting tonight?"

He nodded. "Yeah, I'm hoping it doesn't go too late though."

"Why, you got a date?" she asked in a teasing voice.

"I do," he stated. "I'm meeting Yvonne on the deck afterward."

"Good. I gather things have improved?"

"Things have improved," he declared. "Still not sure quite where we're going yet. I think I have a really good idea, but I thought that the last time too," he admitted. "And I don't want to make a mistake again this time."

She nodded. "I don't think that will be an issue, but I get it. Let's ensure everybody's on the same page."

He smiled and nodded. And, sure enough, as he walked into the meeting, quite a few people were here. Dani was tired, worn out, but getting excited about what was coming her way. By the time the meeting broke up a good hour and a half later, Dennis had cleaned up the table where they'd all been sitting and stepped out on the deck. And, sure enough, tucked into the corner was Yvonne. He walked over quickly. "Hey, I hope I'm not too late tonight."

"You were as late as you needed to be," she replied, waving her arms. "And that's the way life is."

He smiled. "That's a really nice philosophical attitude to take right now. I'll probably have lots of those wedding-related meetings until the big ceremony is over."

"I'm really happy for her," Yvonne said. "I mean, she's done so much for everybody else in her life that it's nice when we can give back."

"Exactly," Dennis agreed. "And what about you?" he asked. "How has your day been?"

"Crazy, chaotic, lovely," she replied, "comfortable. I know that sounds odd to say, but I feel as if I'm back home again, back home in a whole different way. I guess I don't really know how to explain it," she conceded, "but it was good. It was a good day."

"Great. Shane isn't starting you off too hard with those rehab exercises?"

"No, Shane's doing fine." She gave him a smile. "Still, he's certainly checking in on me afterward to ensure that everything I do is not too much."

"Of course he is." Dennis laughed. "I'm sure, in his mind, he doesn't want to be responsible for another setback."

"No, I'm certainly not expecting that in any way. And I'm really glad to hear that you've got the meeting over with and you have time for me tonight."

"Yep, but do you want a cup of tea or something?"

She nodded. "Yeah, let's do that." She pushed her wheelchair toward the coffee station. He put on the teakettle, and she smiled. "A cuppa herbal tea would be good." She noted a couple other people were still milling around in the dining room. "One of the tables has been confiscated for cards, I see." She smiled, as she looked over.

"Yep, when we expanded, we all spelled out how we needed enough meeting room space for everybody to do what they envisioned. We're still not exactly sure that we have the answer to fill all needs, but another expansion would be a problem. So we decided no on a future expansion, at least at this time."

"It doesn't look crowded at the moment," Yvonne noted, as she looked around.

"No, at least for this moment. We may have to add a bigger and separate gathering area later, but, for right now, it's all good."

Chapter 14

YVONNE SMILED, AS she took in just this portion of Hathaway House. "I think it's enough to just accept the fact that you have plans that you need to make and that you have accepted that needs to happen before you worry about more expansion," she suggested. "There's plenty of room for people to eat, to meet, to play cards here in this dining room. Nobody looks crowded, and nobody looks as if they're short on space. If it becomes a problem, Dani should know soon enough."

"I'm not sure how we'll handle it at that future point," he shared, laughing.

She smiled. "The one thing I can count on is you guys figuring it out."

He looked at her, and the smile fell from his face. "Thank you for all these votes of confidence. You've grown so confident in everybody's ability here."

"And I think that's because, although I appreciated everything you guys did for me last time," she explained, "I'm not sure that I really understood exactly how much you did."

"And it wasn't necessary for you to understand, not as the rehab patient here," he pointed out, with a gentle smile. He made their tea and asked, "Do you need a treat to go with your tea?"

"Treats?" she repeated, waggling her eyebrows. "Are

there treats?"

"There are always treats here," he stated, with a smile.

"Like what?"

He shrugged. "Nothing I particularly care for myself, though."

"I never hardly even see you eating," she said. "So, for all I know, you have a secret stash in the backroom."

"I do. Absolutely, I do." And such a solemness filled his tone that she frowned at him. When he laughed, she added, "Oh, no, that's not fair to even think that you guys have something even better than what's displayed out here?"

"How could we possibly?" he protested, chuckling, as he picked up the two cups and carried them outside to the deck, with her rolling along beside him.

"I don't know about that," she began. "That has me thinking that there is actually something better, and I, … I know that that's not really even a thing, is it?"

"No. We share with everybody all the time. If anything, maybe we share too much."

She laughed and nodded. "And it's late, so I don't need food."

"Good enough, but, you know that if you want it …"

"I do know to ask for it this time around."

"Good." Outside, he sat down at the closest table and smiled at her.

She sighed. "It's a beautiful evening. I'm surprised more people aren't out here at this hour of the night."

"Sometimes they are," he replied, looking around, "but it looks as if we have the place to ourselves right now."

"And that's a good thing," she murmured. He looked over at her with an inquiring mind. She shrugged. "I just want to spend time with you." It was obvious he didn't know what to say with that. She smiled. "Fill me in on everything that's happened while I've been gone."

He burst out laughing. "I'm supposed to fill you in on five years, just like that?"

"I was hoping you would," she said, with a smile.

"I dunno how to start," he began. "The days have just gone by, filled with some tears, with some triumphs, with some things that hurt so much that they're just hard to talk about."

She nodded at that. "I can probably match you on tales like that too," she replied. "And we always cry for the failures, but we also always cheer on the successes, right?"

He nodded back. "That's part of life, isn't it? Making sure that we have what we need to carry on to the next day," he murmured. "And it certainly isn't wrong."

"No, I can't imagine anything being wrong about that," she said. "And, when you think about it, … so much is always going on that you just take it day by day."

"Agreed."

"And I, … I should have done more to take things day by day."

"Ah, don't even go down that road. Life is like that. We do the best we can. You get up every day, you do your best, and you go to bed that night and hopefully sleep well." He added, "I saw a video somewhere about a monk, and he said the way to get a good night's sleep was to sleep on a bed of merit." She stopped and stared. He shrugged. "It tickled my fancy at the time, and it's something I've never really forgotten."

"It's a hard thing to forget," she agreed. "I have never heard anything like that, but I really like that."

"When you think about it, we all have that challenge, day in, day out—doing a good job, doing a job that we would be proud of, to do a job of merit," he explained, with a smile. "And I've … It's something I've never forgotten."

She pondered it for a few moments. "I really like it. I wish I could remember these inspirational words when I get down or depressed, or when it feels as if life is against me."

"And sometimes that happens for a reason so that you can cope, so that you don't get so depressed about everything because that onslaught comes sometimes where we're expecting too much out of ourselves."

"Sometimes I feel as if that's every day," she admitted, eyeing him with a wry look.

He nodded, looped his fingers in hers, and said, "Remember to take it one day at a time."

"Yeah, but I do like that idea of merit," she noted. "I just need to remember it when it comes to … I'm very good at forgetting. I start some things, affirmations or what seems to be a good idea at the time, and then I completely forget about it. When I feel as if I've lost something special, I turn around and look for what I've stopped doing, and then I find that weeks have gone by."

"It's not just you either," Dennis stated. "I think that's a common problem with a lot of people. So many people leave here with all these intentions of doing really well and yet don't necessarily follow through," he shared, with a smile. "We don't blame them for it, and we certainly can't blame anybody else. Again, we don't walk that mile in your shoes."

"And yet I think one of the things that got me going was the fact that I always felt as if I had to do more."

"Of course because you always felt that you had to prove yourself."

She nodded. "Not sure I proved it though," she admitted, giving him a wry smile.

"Not sure you had to either," he declared immediately.

She grinned. "That's what I like about you. You always let me off the hook."

"If you need to be let off the hook, then let yourself off the hook on your own," he murmured. "No reason not to."

"And again, you're one of those really nice guys."

He winced. "I heard nice guys finish last, a time or two."

She nodded. "I imagine you have, and I imagine that in so many ways it felt like that the last time."

He stared at her. "We don't need to talk about what happened before."

"Maybe, and yet in some ways I feel as if I do."

"Why?" he asked. "You did what you needed to do for you. Was it hard on me? Yes. Did I blame you for it? No."

"Maybe you should have," she muttered.

"No, that won't get us anywhere," he pointed out, with a gentle smile. "And something I also had to remember was that we did have to work on moving forward ourselves, individually," he shared. "I couldn't take that negative reaction in to the other patients here. That would never have done me any good."

"And I never even think of things like that," she admitted, "or how, when you get down and depressed, it would make everybody around you down and depressed."

"IT'S HARD TO have that problem and be private here at Hathaway House. Of course when you left—and everybody knew that it didn't work out between us—that was hard, but it also showed me how much everybody supported me in at least trying." Her face crumpled. "And I'm not saying that to make you feel bad. Had you been here, you would have been equally supported for your choices."

She shook her head. "My feeling bad for my actions back then isn't your problem either," she murmured. "It just goes to show that I was somebody who needed something else."

"Exactly. What I don't know is whether you're that somebody who still needs something else." She stared at him, and it was obvious she was trying to work her way through what he was saying.

"So are you questioning if I care?" she asked. "Because I thought I had already expressed that."

"You did, but I guess I'm asking … And yet it's not even fair to ask. We should wait until you're a whole lot better, a whole lot more stable, a whole lot more healed, before we even bring up any of this personal stuff."

"Maybe, … yet maybe I would heal faster, if some of this uncertainty was off my plate." He stared at her in surprise. She shrugged. "It certainly feels as if a lot of unresolved issues are between us, and yet I don't think it's so much unresolved as much as we just need to communicate better, honestly and fully."

"Well, I'm never against communicating," Dennis stated. "The question is, what is it that you feel you need to communicate about?"

She winced. "It's always hard."

"I don't know what you mean," Dennis said, slipping back ever-so-slightly so he could face her fully. "I'm totally okay with just seeing if we still like each other, seeing if we want to be friends."

She gave him a misty smile. "And I get that because that's the nice part of you coming out again. I'm not sure I can be so nice."

He frowned at her. "So what are you saying?"

Chapter 15

S HE COULD SENSE his withdrawal almost immediately and realized that, once again, she had caused him pain. She reached out a hand and grabbed his. "I just realized that so many of the things that I did last time caused you hurt and caused me hurt, and I don't want to go there again."

"Meaning that you don't want to go down that relationship pathway?" He nodded. "Okay, if that's what you want."

She shook her head. "I'm not explaining it very well," she muttered. "Or you're being deliberately obtuse." At that, he stared at her in astonishment. Then she burst out laughing. "I know. Most people never say anything negative to you, do they?"

"That's not true," he said, with a small smile. "I've had some very irate interactions here. People have told me to back off. People have told me to keep my New Age dogma to myself, mostly from patients who were having a rough time. However, sometimes even the staff doesn't appreciate something I've said," he admitted. "The fact that you shared a bunch of nice stuff doesn't mean that you can't say some stuff that's not so nice. It's life. I just try to go through every day as if it's one that has meaning for me."

"And it should have meaning for you," she agreed, with a nod. "And I don't think it's fair of anybody to get mad at you."

He burst out laughing. "Everybody has the right to disagree with what I say. And I'm okay with that. I get that sometimes I come across as preachy or whatever else other people might say, but I don't mean to." He shrugged. "Mostly I'm having a good day, and it would be nice to see everybody else have good days."

"Even if they're not trying to?"

"Even if they're not trying to, yes," he agreed. "And sometimes they aren't trying to because they don't know that there is another way. So, if I stay positive and cheerful, maybe it'll make some of them want to be positive and cheerful and to try a little harder."

"And again I have to point out that you really are a nice guy," she murmured. "You don't take offense. You don't do anything that other people can really get offended by, except that sometimes you're too happy."

"Is there such a thing?" he teased, with a lopsided grin.

"Yeah, sometimes I'm sure people out there want to just prick that balloon of happiness of yours because they're having a bad day."

"And because they're having a bad day, I understand," he replied, "because, yeah, I've had bad days too. The day you left was probably the worst day of my life. And I'm not afraid to admit that," he confirmed. "I'm not sad or upset that you know it. It would be wrong to hide it, although I didn't need to bring it to the surface tonight. Still, I'm not sure that I want to go through that hurt again."

"No." She took a deep breath. "So—"

"So?" Dennis repeated, urging her on.

"I—" And she fell silent again.

"So something's bothering you." He reached out a hand for hers. "We're friends. If you need to say something, say something. If I obviously won't like it, I promise I will take it under consideration, and I won't hurt you back for it." He nodded. "I don't want to be the kind of person who hits out if somebody shares something with me that needs to be shared."

She smiled. "I can't imagine. A part of me already wants to go have a hard talk with anybody who says anything mean and nasty to you."

DENNIS STARED AT Yvonne and then burst out laughing. "You always stuck up for everybody else. I was just thinking about that," he murmured. "And when you left, it was because you felt a need to stick up for yourself, and that is and was very important for you." He nodded. "I certainly wouldn't ever hold that against you."

She stared at him. "I forgot about that aspect," she murmured. "I was bad at it, wasn't I?"

"No, you were good at it," he argued. "And you were always there to cheer everybody else on, but somehow you seemed to feel as if, when it came to you, you didn't deserve anybody cheering you on."

"I don't even know if *deserving* was part of it," she murmured thoughtfully. "I think it was more a case of telling myself how I'm capable of doing this, so I should get off my butt and do it. And, even if it was something that knocked me down again and again, I always heard that voice inside me, telling me to stop being a wuss and to get up."

He shrugged. "That critical, pushy voice of yours needs to calm down."

"Yeah, she does. And honestly, it has. In more ways than

it hasn't. I've improved a lot," she declared. "I realized that that was still a lot of the military training I'd gone through, telling me to *Get up, soldier*, that kind of a thing. … Once I realized where that was coming from, it was easy to park it and to tell it to butt out and to let me be me."

"And *being you* is the most important thing," he declared, with a nod.

"It is, and yet being me also means doing a few other things that maybe are a little more unorthodox than I would have expected." He looked at her, one eyebrow raised. She smiled. "See? Last time I hurt you, and it's not something I ever wanted to do. I knew I was doing it, but I, … I felt compelled to leave."

"And so you needed to do that," he agreed, with a nod. "And I'm a big boy. … Rejection's a part of life."

"It is a part of life," she confirmed, looking at him steadily. "The thing is, I was wrong."

He stopped and stared. "In what way?"

"In the way that matters," she muttered, "because you were the most important thing to me back then, and I am so sorry for what I did."

"You didn't do anything," he said gently. "You did what you needed to do at the time to go forward in your life," he explained.

"But I didn't have to hurt you in the process."

"Sure. How else would you do it?" he joked.

"I don't know, but I'm sure there would have been another way."

He shrugged. "As I mentioned, that's all water under the bridge."

"It is. I know that."

"And we don't have to worry about what happened last

time, remember? It's over. You don't have to look backward. Let's look forward."

"And I would like to look forward," she stated. "Matter of fact, I would like to look forward in a big way. I just have to know that we can put … our past behind us."

"Of course we can," he stated. "It would help if I knew what you wanted, but it's way too early for that."

"No, I don't think it's way too early at all." When she saw the stumped look on his face, she added, "It seems like I'm acting hot-cold, hot-cold, but I'm not trying to be that way."

"Good. Nice to know this comes naturally," he teased, with a wry look.

She stared at him in shock, and then her laughter once again bubbled up. "I do love that sense of humor of yours. It made a lot of my time here so much easier."

"Good. Glad that helped."

"And will continue to help," she added, "because obviously I want to spend more time with you."

"I'm glad to hear that, but there is no *obvious* about it."

She stopped and winced, considering his statement. "You know something? You're right." A thought occurred to her, and she studied him for a long moment, realizing that she was at a cusp of something that needed to happen—if she was brave enough. "There is something I do want to ask you," she began slowly, working away through it in her mind.

"Okay. You've always known me to be fully open and honest. So, if you need to ask something, fly at it."

She gave him a lopsided grin. "It's not so easy, and now that I'm on this side of it, I think I finally realized just how hard it was for you and how tough rejection might be."

He stared at her, his gaze steady. "I'm not sure what you're talking about, so ..." And he just left his words hanging.

She nodded and stared off in the distance. "It's a stupid thing, but, by putting myself in your shoes, I can see it so much clearer. And the pain. I'm so sorry."

"Hey, stop. I do not want to rehash all that."

"No, I don't either, and yet I keep doing it." She shook her head. "I really want to go forward, so I need to ask you a very important question."

"Fly at it," he repeated. "Maybe it'll help us get past or through whatever *this* is."

"I hope so," she murmured, "because, of all the things that I hope you realized back then, the most important of all was that I loved you."

"Absolutely. I never doubted that."

She gave him a misty smile. "And I don't know about you, but, for me, love is not something that I say or feel lightly."

He shook his head. "Neither for me. I'm pretty sure we were clear about where we were at back then, too."

"We did talk about it a lot, didn't we?"

He nodded. "We absolutely did, which—" Then he shook his head. "No, there's no *which*."

"Which is why, when I said no to your proposal, it was such a shock," she shared, with a nod.

"You don't have to explain. I should have waited," he said. "I should have let you figure yourself out first."

"Maybe it would've made it easier. I don't know," she muttered. "I was just so bound and determined to get on with life as an independent woman."

"And you did. Don't ever regret that."

"No, I don't regret it. I regret that I went alone," she murmured. "But, for what I had to do, I think at the time it was … the only thing I could do."

He nodded in understanding.

"So the question I have to ask," she began again.

He looked at her expectantly.

"It's stupid because it's literally putting myself in your shoes, and I find I'm absolutely paralyzed right now."

He frowned. "You can ask me anything. I mean, as much as I don't really want to rehash our past, if it will make our future that much easier to be friends or whatever capacity we're talking about here, then you know I'm okay with it. I would prefer to rehash it once and then put it aside and not do it again."

She nodded. "Of course you would," she murmured.

He frowned again.

She smiled and added, "I'm just … I'm not surprised that that's how you would look at it," she noted in a soft tone.

"Okay, now you're worrying me. What's going on here?"

"I'm not even sure what to say about that either," she admitted. "I guess the, … the trick here is just an awful lot is going on in my mind, and one thing just won't leave me alone."

"Okay. And what's that got to do with *right now*?"

"It's that question I want to ask," she replied, "and it hurts."

"You mean, if I've had any relationships while you've been gone?"

She frowned at him. "Of all the things that I could have asked, that one never even occurred to me."

"Oh, okay. So, what is it then?"

"No, now you have to tell me," she said, followed by a nervous laugh.

"The answer is no. There was never anybody else in my life."

Yvonne noted there was almost that *but you* hanging in the air, yet he didn't say it.

Chapter 16

YVONNE COULD UNDERSTAND why, now that she was sitting here, considering what she needed to do, or wanted to do, but wanted to just have it done with. This was not quite how she expected this to go, but then why would he ask her again? It was … It was far too painful.

She sighed. "Look. I know that I did a lot of things that I would choose to do differently next time, and nobody is sadder about this whole thing than I am. And I'm glad that we won't do a postmortem over all this, and that's a good thing because, once we figure out where we're at, maybe we can just move on."

He nodded agreeably. "So, what's still bothering you?"

She smiled. "It's one thing actually and …"

He shook his head at her. "Just spit it out."

She gave him a wry look. "You know, if it was that easy, I *would* just spit it out," she declared. "But somehow it seems immensely hard."

"If it has nothing to do with me having another relationship, I'm not exactly sure … what else could be upsetting you to that extent."

She grabbed his hand, looked down at his strong fingers, his massive palm, and asked, "You know I love you, right?"

He sucked in his breath, but he nodded. "Yes, I know you did love me. I can't imagine that such a love would have disappeared," he replied cautiously.

"No, it didn't disappear. It didn't even go underground," she admitted. "It was always there. It was just there in the back of my head, always waiting, always looking at me, always reminding me of something I walked away from."

"Okay, I'm still not sure what I'm supposed to say to that."

"That's because you're not supposed to say anything," she noted, with the gentlest of smiles. "There are things you can say, but nothing that's expected of you. There is something I am expecting from me though." He just sat and waited. And when he opened his mouth, she held up a hand. "Just give me a moment."

He nodded and settled back… waiting.

She looked down at his hand that she still cradled and began once more, "So I need you to answer me honestly and truthfully, and, yes, you can take time to think about it, if you want," she explained. "First, I'll explain something, and then I'll ask you."

He stared at her, just waiting.

"The first thing is, I need you to understand that I am getting better. I am getting back on my feet. I am not the person I was."

He smiled gently and wanted to say something, but again she held up her hand to ward him off.

"The next thing I need you to understand is, I do have a job. It's probably not the same job I'll stick with, but it is a job. Dani approached me originally about working here as a full-time IT person, and, if I get that opportunity again, I would be delighted to take her up on it," Yvonne shared, with a smile. "And somewhere along the line, down the road maybe, I can see changing pretty well everything, even what

I'm doing for a career, mostly because I need to do something that feeds my soul and not just my bank account."

"Oh, I can understand that," he agreed.

She smiled and then started to laugh. "Yes, you of all people would understand that. So I have a big question to ask you." She leaned forward to face him, so that she could see right into his expression and hopefully read the truth there. She found an inner strength she hadn't ever expected at this moment in time, when she continued. "I have to ask …" She hesitated, and then whispered, "Will you marry me?"

DENNIS STARED AT her in shock. Whatever he'd thought she would ask, he'd started to worry what other mess she'd dreamt up in her heart of confusion. But that was not what she was focused on. Never in his wildest dreams had he ever thought this would come about. He swallowed hard.

Yvonne whispered, "Is that a no?"

And then her previous words about being in his position—realizing how hard it was and how bad rejection was— hit him, as he realized that she was expecting a no right back. He shook his head. "Of all the things that you could have asked me, *that* is not anything I was prepared for."

"That's still not a yes or a no," she pointed out.

He gave her the gentlest of smiles. "And I never expected to be asked."

"I know, but I figured that, this time, all the risk should be on my part."

"And there shouldn't be any risk," he noted.

"True, and yet somehow a truly big risk *is* involved. I'm

letting you know how I care about you immensely and how much you are a major part of my life and how much I want you back in my life again in a big way, and, no, I don't want it on a temporary basis. I want to go back to when I told you no five years ago, and I want to redo all that," she explained. "I don't know why I did what I did, but I presume I needed to. So, I'm here now to tell you that, whatever that was back then, it's over, and I'm so desperate to be a part of your life again," she whispered. "I'm just hoping that you want to be a part of mine."

He nodded. Inside was this slow blossom, a healing from inside that he didn't even realize he'd needed. "Are you sure?"

She chuckled. "Isn't that my line?"

"Maybe," he said, with a lopsided grin. "I have to admit I wasn't prepared for this."

"I'm not sure we can ever be prepared," she stated, with a knowing smile. "I wasn't prepared when you asked me either."

"No, I don't imagine you were," he agreed. "I just knew you were leaving, and I wanted to ensure that you knew how I felt."

"And I knew how you felt," she replied, "but I couldn't let you stop me."

"Got it," he muttered, with a smile.

"And you still haven't answered my question," she whispered.

He looked at her and saw that she was at the point of tears. He reached over and scooped her out of her wheelchair easily. She was small compared to him, even though she was tall for a woman. And he sat her in his lap and whispered, "Thank you for the honor and the request. My answer is, of course, absolutely yes. You've always been in my heart, and you have forever been part of my soul," he whispered. "I just had to wait for you to come back and find me."

"And I'm here," she whispered, tears in her eyes, as she clutched her arms around his neck and held on tight. "Dear God, that was so hard."

He smiled and nodded. "It is, indeed. Probably harder for you than it was for me because I was so sure that I knew what your answer would be, and yet it wasn't." She winced at that again. "And again"—he placed a finger against her lips—"it doesn't matter. We have just taken a turn on a completely new and different path. If you ever change your mind again, it'll break my heart."

"I have no intention of changing my mind. You have always been exactly where you are right now—in my heart. I just want to go forward, knowing that this is the pathway that we both want."

"Exactly." He looked down at her and grinned. "Considering that you've never proposed before, you did a great job."

She smiled, leaned up against him, and whispered, "Thank you. … You do realize I've got months of rehab to go."

He nodded. "Yep, you sure do," he stated cheerfully. "Just means we have months before you can walk down the aisle."

"And if I want to wheel down the aisle?"

He shrugged. "Then you can wheel down the aisle. That's your choice."

She grinned. "Once again, you're just way too easy to get along with."

"No, because I also know that you won't want the wedding pictures down the road to be of you in a wheelchair, so I know you'll work to get to that point."

"You're right, and I never even thought of that."

"Just don't push yourself so hard that you set yourself back."

She gave him a smirk. "I think I've learned that lesson already *this* time."

He chuckled. "An awful lot of Dani's wedding details are going on around me at the moment and an awful lot of bride-to-be emotions, even from our beloved Dani. So, I'm a little bit more in tune with that than I had expected to be."

"I'm glad to hear that because I've never been married before, and I don't know how to do weddings," she shared. "I just know I want to spend the rest of my life with you."

"And I'm really glad to hear that." He wrapped her up in his arms, lowered his head, and, just before his lips took hers, he whispered, "Welcome home."

ZANDER TOLSTON WATCHED out the window of the ambulance—or interfacility transfer or whatever they called this—as it pulled up to a ramp.

When the back doors opened, his attendant smiled at him and announced, "You've arrived."

"Glad to hear it," he muttered, controlling his pain.

He looked at the big building that he'd spent months and months getting accepted into. His military teammate and hospital room partner, Xavier, had already left after his rehab time at Hathaway House but had promised to come visit. Apparently a wedding was happening a few months from now, but all kinds of plans for it were still ongoing.

Zander just wanted rehab plans for himself. He hoped the wedding wouldn't detract from getting the care he needed here, but he was prepared to trust what everybody had told him—that Hathaway House was the place where he needed to be. He'd wanted to come for so long, and now he was here. It seemed to be a miracle. He looked around as he was helped out of the transport vehicle and into a wheelchair.

Even as he sat down again, the pain jarred him throughout his body. He had survived his injuries, but he had broken his pelvis, both legs, and several ribs. Multiple surgeries had attended to his pelvis and legs. His ribs had been wrapped and took forever to heal. Even now, if he took too deep of a breath, several ribs reminded him that they were still in flux. Plus, his weakened immunity also kept him down. He blew out a huge exhale.

"We'll get you inside and get you settled," the attendant said. "You'll be just fine."

"I hope so," Zander replied, looking around. "Hathaway's way bigger than I thought."

"They did a massive expansion recently," the attendant shared, "which is a good thing, since the demand for this place is insane."

"As long as they keep up the good work," he murmured.

"I haven't heard anything to the contrary. Everybody I know of who's here, or who has been here, loves it."

"That's good to hear. I have a good friend who came through this place, and he's already come and gone. I was hoping to be here … before he left, but he did amazingly well."

"I think a lot of people do amazingly well here," the guy noted, as he wheeled Zander up the ramp. "And I suspect you will too."

Zander looked over, grateful for the vote of confidence. "Maybe. It seems as if I've been a sickly child for a very long time."

"You're not a child now, and, after what you've been through, I don't think anybody'll see you in that light."

"That would be good too," he noted, with a smile, as he looked around. "It's quite the place, isn't it?"

"It is. Now here you go, up and in through the front door."

And, with that, he was pushed into a reception area. A group of people stood around.

One woman detached herself, walked over, and greeted him. "Hey. What's your name?"

"Zander, Zander Tolston."

"And you are the arrival I've been waiting for," she murmured. She reached out a hand to shake his and introduced herself. "Nelly, the nutritionist here. And I understand that we have some immunity to build up with you."

"Yeah, you could say that. I seem to catch everything going around."

"That's okay," she murmured. "We'll get you fixed up just right." At that, she motioned at another woman, calling out to her, "Dani."

This was Dani, the woman who managed the place. Yet she looked way too young for the job title. Her smile that came his way was electric.

"Hi," she said. "Welcome to Hathaway. We do have your room ready, so let's get you in and settled right away."

As Nelly wheeled him to his room, and Dani walked alongside him, he looked around and shared, "Xavier told me a lot about this place."

"That's good to hear," Dani replied. "You should feel right at home. Plus, you'll see him sometime soon, I'm sure. He's no longer a rehab patient, but we see him often."

"He told me about his time here, and I'm really happy for him. He did way better than he expected."

"A lot of people do," she murmured. "And you might find that that'll be the same for you too."

"I hope so. Right about now, I have to admit I'm not feeling 100 percent."

"Nope, nobody is when they first get here," Dani stated, "and the change can be overwhelming very quickly."

He nodded. "I can see that. I'm not sure why, but just a

lot is going on."

"And nothing is important for you to figure out right now," she noted, "except to rest. We'll give you the tools that you need to contact any of us, and Nelly here will get you a nutritional shake full of vitamins and minerals to help bolster your system. We have orders from your doctors to ensure that we do the best we can to add some weight to you and to get your immune system strengthened."

"Yeah, that would be helpful," Zander agreed, "not to mention getting me back on my feet and, with any luck, back to living a normal life."

"We'll do everything we can," Nelly declared in a bright, cheerful voice.

He looked over at her. "Aren't you awfully young. Both of you actually."

Nelly laughed. "Is twenty-nine *awfully young*?"

He nodded. "It seems sometimes, yes."

"Maybe," she conceded. "And how old are you?"

"Thirty-three," he replied, "and I feel as if I've lost twenty future years of a potential healthy life just because of all the injuries."

"Injuries can totally set you back," she declared. "So we'll have to ensure that the rest of the years you have are at peak performance."

"Oh, I like the sound of that," he muttered, looking at her in surprise.

She smiled. "Hey, we're here to help. Follow our instructions, trust us, and give us a chance, and we'll do the best for you that we can."

And, with that, he was pushed into a private room with its own bath. He frowned. "I get a room to myself?"

"You do," Dani confirmed. "And, yes, you're special, but

we do try to give everybody a private room, just like your friend Xavier had one."

"I did hear about that. I just figured he was lucky."

"He was very lucky," Nelly stated, with a smile. "But you're here now, in our hands, and that makes you lucky too."

He looked up, and, for the first time in a long time, he almost believed her. He nodded. "In that case, bring it on."

This concludes Book 25 of Hathaway House: Yvonne.
Read about Zander: Hathaway House, Book 26

Hathaway House: Zander (Book #26)

Welcome to Hathaway House. Rehab Center. Safe Haven. Second chance at life and love.

Zander finds it hard to believe he's finally made it to Hathaway House—months after Xavier came here. Although his friend is still here to greet him on his arrival, Zander's essentially on his own. Seeing the contrast between Xavier before and now is amazing. His success should be something that springboards Zander to follow in his friend's footsteps, but Zander's frail health is always there in the background, holding him back.

Nelly, a recently hired nutritionist, is thrilled to be at Hathaway House and seeing Zander's weak body reminds her of all the reasons she went into this field. He's desperately in need of every bit of help that the staff here can provide. Just to add to the chaos, a large wedding is being organized for Dani and Aaron.

For Zander, seeing the happy couple reminds him of all that's missing in his life and all that just might be here for him, if he can but reach out for it.

Find Book 26 here!
To find out more visit Dale Mayer's website.
https://geni.us/DMSZander

Author's Note

Thank you for reading Yvonne: Hathaway House, Book 25! If you enjoyed the book, please take a moment and leave a short review.

Dear reader,

I love to hear from readers, and you can contact me at my website: www.dalemayer.com or at my Facebook author page. To be informed of new releases and special offers, sign up for my newsletter or follow me on BookBub. And if you are interested in joining Dale Mayer's Reader Group, here is the Facebook sign up page.
http://geni.us/DaleMayerFBGroup

Cheers,
Dale Mayer

About the Author

Dale Mayer is a *USA Today* best-selling author, best known for her SEALs military romances, her Psychic Visions series, and her Lovely Lethal Garden cozy series. Her contemporary romances are raw and full of passion and emotion (Broken But … Mending, Hathaway House series). Her thrillers will keep you guessing (Kate Morgan, By Death series), and her romantic comedies will keep you giggling (*It's a Dog's Life*, a stand-alone novella; and the Broken Protocols series, starring Charming Marvin, the cat).

Dale honors the stories that come to her—and some of them are crazy, break all the rules and cross multiple genres!

To go with her fiction, she also writes nonfiction in many different fields, with books available on résumé writing, companion gardening, and the US mortgage system. All her books are available in print and ebook format.

Connect with Dale Mayer Online

Dale's Website – www.dalemayer.com
Twitter – @DaleMayer
Facebook Page – geni.us/DaleMayerFBFanPage
Facebook Group – geni.us/DaleMayerFBGroup
BookBub – geni.us/DaleMayerBookbub
Instagram – geni.us/DaleMayerInstagram
Goodreads – geni.us/DaleMayerGoodreads
Newsletter – geni.us/DaleNews